Soulmate

Also by Deepak Chopra

Soulmate

Deepak Chopra

NEW AMERICAN LIBRARY

New American Library
Published by New American Library, a division of
Penguin Putnam Inc., 375 Hudson Street,
New York, New York 10014, U.S.A.
Penguin Books Ltd, 80 Strand,
London WC2R 0RL, England
Penguin Books Australia Ltd, Ringwood,
Victoria, Australia
Penguin Books Canada Ltd, 10 Alcorn Avenue,
Toronto, Ontario, Canada M4V 3B2
Penguin Books (N.Z.) Ltd, 182–190 Wairau Road,
Auckland 10, New Zealand

Penguin Books Ltd, Registered Offices:
Harmondsworth, Middlesex, England

Published by New American Library, a division of Penguin Putnam Inc.
Previously published in a G. P. Putnam's Sons edition.

First New American Library Printing, October 2002
10 9 8 7 6 5 4 3 2 1

 REGISTERED TRADEMARK—MARCA REGISTRADA

New American Library Trade Paperback ISBN: 0-451-20704-1

The Library of Congress has catalogued the hardcover edition of this title as follows:

Chopra, Deepak.
Soulmate
p.   cm.
ISBN 0-399-14798-5
1. Psychiatrists—Fiction.   2. New York (N.Y.)—Fiction.
3. Spiritual life—Fiction.
I. Title
PS3553.H587S66   2001   2001019731
813'.54—dc21

Printed in the United States of America

Book design by Chris Welch

To my father

You split me, and tore my heart open.

You filled me with love.

You poured your spirit into mine.

Now I know you as I know myself.

—FROM THE *ODES OF SOLOMON*

Part One

Romance

1.

Romance is the passport to a mystery.

—Raj Rabban's journal

Anyone who believes in love should hear the story of Raj Rabban. At twenty-five he had yet to fall in love. In fact he barely knew what it took. Work was his excuse, as so often happens. Raj had been working for some time in a Manhattan emergency room. His constant companions were gunshot-wound victims who bled out on the table, overdosed addicts found by the police, and highly successful suicide attempts. In medical school, he had tenderly watched over the needs of a corpse for several months, so while dating, if he had time for it, he carried a faint whiff of formaldehyde. Literally. Girls smelled it on his fingers even after he scrubbed his hands raw.

To be honest, the greatest love that Raj had experienced was reflected in his mother's eyes when he was three. Amma treated him like a cross between a divine blessing and a Mogul prince. His favorite dessert as a child was warm carrot halvah covered with a thin leaf of edible silver foil.

"And one last piece for you," she would say, sticking a bright sliver on his forehead. She had even named him Rajah.

Raj learned that baby princes have a hard time making the transition to normal adults. He didn't want to be adored forever. Not just adored, that is. Finally he gave his parents the gift of enormous relief when he found someone. Actually, they found her for him, but they were relieved just the same. She was a good and beautiful woman, and she cared for him. Daddy-ji told her she would be marrying the whole family.

"Do the right thing, don't break your mother's heart," Daddy-ji said to Raj when they all came together for a party on Shivaratri. Raj wasn't that sure where his mother stood. Every promising girl was the right one until they got too close. As for this girl, Raj was beginning to love her. Just not enough.

"How about tonight?" his father said on Devali, the festival of lights.

"Not tonight," said Raj. He had no intention of breaking anyone's heart, and he loved the girl more each day. But Raj had to look after his own future, or what would he have to offer her? Being patient as well as good, the girl agreed. There was no hurry.

By Christmas, Raj felt differently. The girl came into focus as someone he cherished. Her name became real to him. Maya. She was no longer just the girl his family wanted him to marry. Maya was his, and the thought of having to wait became intolerable.

It wouldn't matter, though. What Raj didn't know was that he was being pursued. Love and death were like two sisters, one beautiful, the other terrifying, that fate had joined. Both had set eyes on Raj, only he saw the beautiful sister first while ignoring the one that followed her a step behind.

The beautiful one was named Molly. Raj met her on the New York subway that summer. It was hard to miss her—she was the fiery redhead in the pink wedding dress. Raj had trudged on at Forty-second Street, the Grand Central Station stop, lugging two battered suitcases on his way home from vacation. He already had four messages on his machine from Maya, and he was anxious to reach her.

It was muggy and hot, the kind of dog day in August that is hard to suffer through, even without luggage. The bride was hanging on to a strap, afraid to sit down for fear of ruining her long satin skirt, which was at the first stage of rumpling into damp creases. Their eyes met, she looked away. He didn't. For one thing, she was a startling vision to stumble upon underground.

"Do you need any help?" he asked, making sure that his tone sounded soothing rather than suspicious.

The girl raised her eyebrows. "Not as much as you," she said. Raj was muscular, but the two battered suitcases were carrying half his textbooks from the past three years and some clothes Maya left with him when she had to leave the lake cottage early. It was their first vacation alone. They had spent much of the time talking about their upcoming wedding.

As Raj looked on, a couple of punks bumped into the girl shoving their way onto the train. "Watch it," she warned without purpose. A small nosegay of orchids was knocked off her wrist, its silk ribbon undone. She picked it up, examined it a second, then tossed it away. As she ducked impatiently to look out the window, a panoply of red hair was flung back over her shoulders. Raj could feel its liquid motion as if it were brushing against his skin. He was disturbed to feel such a thing.

"Come on, come on," the girl muttered.

He leaned across the aisle, deflecting the shuffle of bodies milling between them. "Are you late for your wedding?" The metal doors would slam closed any minute, and then the clatter of the tracks would make it impossible to hear anything.

The girl noticed him again, and this time she didn't turn away. "It's not my wedding," she said. "I'm a bridesmaid, and my car broke down. I had no other choice." She pointed upward with her chin. "And I guess you don't get married too often. Brides wear white. You get your reputation back for a day." A smile broke through her mask of worry. A stunning smile.

The doors to the train didn't close and after a few minutes the conductor announced that there was a track fire farther up the line and all uptown traffic would be delayed indefinitely.

Raj laughed. "You're screwed," he yelled over the groans of the other passengers. "How far do you have to go, anyway?"

Cathedral of St. John the Divine, she told him, all the way uptown. He got the picture: frantic bridesmaid stuck in midtown traffic with a beat-up car that dies at the worst possible moment. Unable to resuscitate it, she ditches and runs.

"Come with me," Raj shouted. He abandoned the two battered suitcases, clawing his way around half a dozen gray suits. He would act on the assumption that she was a free spirit. Good assumption, as it turned out. On the platform he picked his way through the crowd and made it to the stairs. He should have expected that the girl hadn't followed him, but she had. It was an incredible act of faith, really.

"Now what?" she asked.

"Just run up the stairs, if you can in that dress."

"Don't worry about it." Her face was flushed, but her eyes were amused, probably at him. Raj turned and led the way. They emerged on the south side of Grand Central. A flock of yellow taxis waited at the hotel next door, and a minute later they were huddled, panting but victorious, in the backseat of one, racing up Park Avenue.

"Cut across the park," Raj ordered, not even caring when the Pakistani driver gave him a look that said, "Buddy, there's no other way but to cut across the park."

"Be careful not to sit on my lace. There's tons of it," the girl warned.

"They're going to impound your car, you know," said Raj.

She shrugged. "What will they do with your suit-cases? I'm Molly, I don't think I told you, and I feel ridiculous. Bridesmaids don't carry money. I had to plead with someone to give me subway fare."

"I'm Raj—short for Rajah."

"I thought you looked exotic. That's a compliment, by the way. You're from—?"

"India, but I came over here as a kid."

"I knew an Indian girl at school. Just the one. You're my second."

"There are a lot of us."

Molly looked over the driver's shoulder, her face worried again. The wedding occupied her mind much more than Raj did, however exotic he might be. An irrational male instinct made Raj believe that it was up to him to get the traffic to move. He cursed every double-parked delivery truck and felt his neck muscles knotting whenever the driver lurched to a halt, cut off by a more wily cab. Molly slumped back onto the torn black leather seat, yards of lace bunched in her lap. She was resigned now, whatever happened.

She said, "I just remembered something ridiculously obvious. Weddings don't have intermissions, so being an hour late is the same as five minutes." She seemed to notice him now. "I'm going to have to think of a way to make this up to you. It's huge," she said.

"You can buy me a drink," he said. "And maybe I can bring my fiancée."

"Ah, fair warning," said Molly. "When did you get engaged?"

"We're not yet. It's an almost, but 'fiancée' makes her feel more secure."

Cabs, like dentist's chairs and hair salons, provoke riskless intimacy with strangers. The two soon hit on a wavelength, talking about the Troubles, her charter flight to Paris that summer, his hole of an apartment on the edge of Spanish Harlem that no respectable woman should ever be forced to enter for fear of death by disgust.

"I won't ask you if you're related to the Gandhis," she said.

"Thanks. I won't ask you if your relatives built bombs for the IRA in Belfast." Her last name, Mahoney, told Raj where her people were from. It turned out that they had drifted almost accidentally from County Mayo to Kansas City. Still the cab was nowhere near the church. So they talked about the uncanny similarity between hell and New York in August, her pious grandmother who went to mass every day, his pious grandmother who had defended her house with an old army pistol during the Hindu-Muslim riots of 1947.

"About my Indian girlfriend in college," said Molly. "Well, I was just a hick. I thought she was Puerto Rican when we met. I guess that's an offensive thing to say."

"It won't win you any peace prizes," Raj said tolerantly.

Raj found himself watching Molly's small gestures with fascination: the flick of a hand to pull back wayward hair when it covered her right ear though not her left, for some reason. The restless drumming of fingers that were used to holding a purse or a knapsack. The flash of a smile that was almost immediately taken back, as if something too personal had been recklessly thrown away on a stranger.

"So, this is your first year as a real doctor?" asked Molly.

"Right, I'm an intern this year, and then I'll be a resident." Molly touched her hair, and Raj had the sensation again that he could feel the softness of it on his skin. He said, "But you have to pretend to be a real doctor on rounds while you are still in school."

"Which means you're fooling people," she observed, frowning.

"You could look at it that way, but it also gives patients a sense of confidence while you sew up the gash they made with a kitchen knife or try to explain why taking their angina medicine really is important." Raj didn't want her to be disappointed in him. "It reassures them."

"But you're still fooling them," she said.

"Okay. Now I'm becoming a psychiatrist," he said, "but you might not think they're real doctors, either." That was certainly how his parents felt.

"Psychiatry?" Daddy-ji had moaned. "I dare you to find a way for a doctor to cure fewer people and make less money trying."

Raj's mother had cried until there were dark rings under her eyes before she ran out to get something to touch them up.

Raj and Molly hardly noticed when the cab pulled up to the church.

"Well, I guess this is me," Molly said doubtfully, peering out the window in case she might see some other members of the wedding party. But the cathedral steps were empty except for a few homeless people stretched out under dirty blankets, staking out the best spots before nightfall.

"You better run," said Raj, digging into his pocket for a wad of crumpled bills. Molly hadn't opened the door, so he reached over and got it for her. He was careful not to let his sweaty bare arm brush her pink dress. "Why aren't you getting out?" he asked.

Molly tapped her watch. It had taken forty minutes to get there. She pointed to the empty steps. "I see your point. I guess I was hoping you really liked talking to me," Raj said, "and you just couldn't pull yourself away."

The cocky remark surprised her, and she laughed. "You're not that lucky, Rajah," she said, and then she leaned over and gave him a kiss—close enough to his mouth and just long enough so that he would remember it—before jumping out of the cab. "But at least you were a little lucky."

She took a step back, removed her shoes, and turned to run into the church. Raj watched her make the huge portal doors two steps at a time before she disappeared into the darkness of the sanctuary. *She thinks she's going to make it anyway*, he thought. Molly had told him that she was an aspiring actress who had been in a couple of productions. *Now she can make her entrance*, Raj thought, imagining that she would do it very well.

MAYA WASN'T IRRITATED that Raj called an hour late. "Of course brides don't wear pink," she said, laughing at Raj's story. "Was she beautiful?"

"I guess the word would be 'striking,' not 'beautiful,' " Raj lied.

"You have a gallant streak," Maya said. They agreed to meet for dinner at the end of the week.

Interns work thirty-six hours on and twelve off, a grind that took all of Raj's concentration. He found himself thinking about the redhead from the subway only late at night when he was stretched out on a folding cot in the interns' lounge. Scattered thoughts, but persistent. They gave him something to do as he was drifting off to sleep besides staring at the yellow stains in the plaster ceiling and seeing lobes of the cerebral cortex. Or wondering where he was really going.

His parents came from a culture that teaches surrender as life's highest goal, and even Raj, a stepchild of America, had vaguely absorbed the lesson. Not that he could embrace it. Early lessons from his upbringing ran through his head. Surrender meant detachment. It meant placing who you are as the highest mystery. In simplest terms it meant putting your soul first and the world second. Daddy-ji held a humble place, but more than once he had taken Raj aside and told him about his beliefs: The man who surrenders is always open, always observing. You seek detachment not so that nothing can touch you, but so that you have enough space to find out what is real.

Didn't Christ teach us, in this new, strange land, to be in the world but not of it?

Raj did the opposite without even thinking about it. He seized the world with both hands, and his deepest fear was that he might not be of it enough. He knew a dozen Indian kids who were exactly the same. If surrender is an empty vessel for grace to fill, Raj spent many days feeling empty enough. What would fill him remained a question.

For the moment he could throw himself into trauma work in the ER, and ahead lay psychiatry. To get a head start Raj hung around the chief resident in psychiatry. The medical students called him Baron Bruno. He was burly and bearded, and he reminded everyone of a professional wrestler. His real name, a surprisingly mild one, was Clarence. Clarence lumbered, but he was the guy you wanted on your side when someone went berserk on crack in the waiting room. It was Clarence who allowed him to do workups on disturbed patients dumped by the police. Every workup started routinely with a physical exam but turned into a brief psych evaluation.

"Make it brief but sharp," Clarence advised. "You're the first face they see when they hit the beach, and the first opinion everyone is going to rely on later."

"You're trusting my judgment?" asked Raj nervously.

He had only gone through one psych rotation in the hospital since medical school.

"No, I'm trusting the *Physician's Desk Reference,*" remarked Clarence. "Keep it simple. Look up the menu of tranquilizers and antidepressants in the PDR. Except for bonkers and flamers and anyone else who is presented with hallucinations, those meds are what you'll be relying on ninety percent of the time. Find the standard dosage and then prescribe half of that."

"Half?" asked Raj.

"It's safer. These people have damaged machinery already. Let's not turn it into total mush."

"Deal," said Raj. They both knew that the chief resident was required by the rules to check any scrip that Raj wrote, so he felt protected.

The challenges could bury you. "What are we really doing for these people?" Raj asked in front of the vending machine that dispensed black coffee, jelly doughnuts, and chips. A suicidal teenager had been admitted to the psych wards, routine after an overdose, but this one's parents had screamed in his face and almost spit on him when they discovered that keeping their daughter in restraints for twenty-four hours was mandatory.

"As long as you don't know the answer to that question, you'll survive as a psychiatrist," Clarence said, pulling the lever for stale Twinkies.

"You're saying that ignorance will be my motivation?" Raj asked.

"I'm saying that all freaks are people, and all people are freaks. It's a cosmic equation you'll spend the rest of your life trying to solve."

Raj's parents caught him at the apartment two weeks later and announced on the phone that it was time for him to choose a priest from the temple for his wedding with Maya. Besides the ceremony, which would include a sacred fire, rice, and ghee, a white horse for the groom and a litter for the bride, there were the charts. Who was going to do their astrological charts?

"No white horse," said Raj. "We're not in Delhi. It would bankrupt you, and I'll feel ridiculous."

"I was joking," Daddy-ji said. "We just don't want you to wait anymore."

"Maya smiles too much when I see her," observed Amma. "I'm sure she's secretly miserable."

Raj couldn't offer a good excuse as to why he hadn't attended to the wedding details. Or why he hadn't simply let Maya take over, since she was willing and capable.

His father grew more impatient. "You've lost your mind. This is a nice girl."

Daddy-ji had run a small neighborhood grocery in Queens almost since coming to this country. He felt no

need to peer beyond his impeccably arranged vegeta-
bles, deli sandwiches, cigarettes, daisy bouquets, cold
cuts, and pyramids of fruit. Other fathers in the neighborhood worshiped the NFL draft or the Yankees
pitching lineup, but Raj learned early on that his father
was different. His personal deities were the gods of tidi-
ness, cautious markups, and keeping an eye on the kids
near the magazine racks. Modest gods, like himself.

"I love her, she loves me, so stop pushing the elephant," Raj told Daddy-ji.

Raj was only half-listening to his father while riffling
through the Sunday *Times* before throwing it down the
garbage chute. His eye caught a name: Mary Mahoney.
His heart missed a beat. It was an ad for a hit play, a full
page topped with fulsome praise from the critics. Raj
looked closer. *Ah, Wilderness.* He felt goose bumps on
his arm. "Hold on. Daddy, isn't Molly short for Mary?"
Raj asked.

"We don't know any girls named Molly."

Maya called an hour later, setting a time for dinner.
She had a late class, but she could meet him on Fifty-
sixth Street at one of the Indian cafés. Raj asked if she'd
like to go to a play afterward.

"*Cats?*"

"No, a legitimate play. Eugene O'Neill," said Raj.

The ad was open in front of him. He noticed the name of a famous young Hollywood star burning brightly above the title of the play. Molly, if it was actually her, shared the second line with two other actors. It seemed impressive, more than an actress might usually deserve after only a couple of productions.

Maya showed up ten minutes late at the Bombay Café off Seventh Avenue. Raj, waiting at the bar with a beer, thought that of all the single women who had passed through the door, most on the dreary mission of blind dates arranged by Indian parents, Maya was the beauty. She wore slightly silvery lipstick and a smart two-piece outfit, not a sari. She was of Punjabi background with large, sympathetic eyes and pale, desirable skin, which Raj didn't dwell on. His family had originally come from South India in the dying twilight of the Raj. Daddy-ji was vague about their wanderings, perhaps because it was a tale worth hiding, but his darker skin made him sensitive in the North as a child.

At school Daddy-ji cringed whenever some fourth-form boys would rail, "Not black, not white, but khaki." This taunt was reserved for one of the Anglo-Indians waiting to be picked last for football. Raj didn't think about skin that way, but he had a lingering hint of the old stigma.

"The off-ramps were a nightmare," Maya apologized. She was out of breath from running three blocks from the parking garage off Tenth Avenue.

"How was the case?" asked Raj, signaling the head-waiter that they wanted their table.

"Very sad. Three young children under the age of five. The mother isn't a bad woman, but they're going to take them away from her." As they sat down by the window, Maya put her briefcase under the table. She was getting her master's in social work at Columbia and she worked part-time as a youth advocate. Twice a week she attended court hearings for abandoned children.

"Did you testify for the mother?" asked Raj. They were brought large red plastic menus to study. He didn't need to. "Rgan josh," he said. Maya had the fish vindaloo.

"I wasn't there to give an opinion, just to verify the home situation. It's bad. The mother can't afford day care, the father just went to jail. It's not her fault that the kids got out of the yard and wandered too far," said Maya.

"Whose fault was it if not hers?" asked Raj.

"I know, I know," Maya sighed. She often got overly attached to the cases she observed. Raj suspected that

Maya might even be offering these people help on her own time. She was that good. When the food came, Maya began eating with her fingers, tearing off bits of chapati bread as a scoop for the rice and curried fish. Raj automatically picked up a fork. Unlike Raj, Maya had been born in America, her parents having come over so that her father could find better prospects in his engineering work.

She had been astonished when Raj told her that he had never set foot in India since childhood. "How could you not go?" she said in the tone of someone who has just heard that you didn't visit a dying relative in the hospital. Maya herself had taken summers off in New Delhi or Bombay since the age of twelve.

"But I never joined the South Asian societies in school," she said. "It's demeaning to keep moaning over who we are. I don't care about the Tamil Tigers in Sri Lanka or the corruption of politicians or whomever."

Raj immediately admired her for this. Like him, she wasn't obsessed with belonging or not belonging. "When you go back, does any of the spiritual side tempt you?" he asked.

"Tempt me? Maybe," she said, "but I wouldn't know what to look for. Naked sadhus begging on the street? Gurus consulted by corporations before a big takeover?

In my family, the purpose of life is to nurse grievances and grab as much money as possible. Nothing makes us more Indian than that."

"But you're different?"

"Of course. That's what I tell myself. Just like you."

Raj laughed and felt easy. Unlike the other dates that his parents had arranged, Maya was neither timid nor desperate. From their first meeting, she had been honest, and she hadn't treated Raj like a stranger sharing a soon-to-be-forgotten evening with another stranger. Other women just focused on not acting so bizarre, needy, or frank that they turned into an object of ridicule the next day. He never got to see what they were really like.

Maya looked out the window at the passing parade. "We don't belong because of where we are. We belong because of *who* we are."

"And who are you?" asked Raj.

"Part of this." She waved her hand at the throng outside. "And part of something else."

THE PLAY MUST have been a genuine hit. They pushed through a packed throng pouring from limos and cabs; furred matrons on foot were looking down so as not to poke a spiked heel through a grate in the sidewalk, while their husbands impatiently nudged from behind. Raj caught Molly's name on the poster outside and hoped that Maya didn't notice his excitement. A moment later, they were seated, and the curtain came up.

And there she was. Molly didn't play a minor character passing coffee in the drawing room or filling out a pack of picnickers in Act II. She was the female lead, a winsome, comically vexed girl in love with her equally winsome opposite. Raj was mesmerized and surprisingly frightened—he felt as if Molly were walking a tightrope and he had to hold his breath to keep her from falling. She was in no danger, though. Molly had every gesture under control. The coy sidelong glance that she cast was not her real-life glance but a perfectly calculated effect. Like the lilting quaver in her voice that signified maiden innocence and the shy heave of a bosom that attracted thoughts of Eros without giving in to them.

Maya leaned over and whispered, "She's so good. How does anyone learn that?"

Raj didn't know. He could feel this <u>ethereal</u> character on stage, but Molly remained something else for him, the flesh he had been pressed next to in the cab, the faint breath he sensed when she leaned over as the car lurched around a corner on its busted shocks. The physical memory made his face warm. He felt a pang when the young lovers kissed.

At intermission Raj didn't want to get up from his seat, but Maya was fascinated by Guy, the Hollywood heartthrob. "He's a fox. Especially opposite the girl. She could be on *Masterpiece Theater*," Maya enthused.

Raj barely heard what she said. Something was happening to him.

"I'm sorry," said Maya. "Am I being too suburban?"

"Not at all." Raj jumped out of his seat. "Who needs a drink?"

The heat and crush of bodies in the narrow lobby made Raj light-headed. At the bar he ordered a Scotch straight up. He glanced over at Maya. "And a spritzer," he added.

"Only if it's for you, sweetie. I'm fine," Maya said, and when she looked away, Raj let her be. The person dominating his thoughts was Molly, shimmering under white key lights and gauzy blue gels of moonlight. Raj had to see her again. The surge of desire had come instantly, and it was irresistible.

"Can you take this?" he said, handing his drink to Maya.

"Why?"

"I think I heard my beeper. There are too damn many in here; I almost missed it. Let me go outside."

Maya looked disappointed, fearing that he would be pulled back on call. Raj promised not to leave unless it was an absolute emergency. "I'll be back in two minutes; you go in. If I miss the curtain, I'll wait for you on the Broadway side."

Maya hesitated. The five-minute bell had rung, and only a few stragglers remained in the lobby. Raj willed her to go, and after giving him a kiss and a pained smile, she did.

Feeling strangely excited, Raj burst out the door and spied a flower seller setting up under the marquee on Broadway. The man was pulling cellophane-wrapped roses from the back of a van. Raj fished a twenty out of his pocket.

"I'll take six," he said.

The man glanced at the dangling bill without pausing. "That will buy you four, pal," he said. Raj took them and ran back inside. He passed the ushers and fell back on instinct. One of the side doors looked promising. He would have to trust that it didn't just open on a closet—it didn't. Beyond was darkness and some kind of passage lit by bare lightbulbs. Raj dashed down it, holding his breath and hoping that no one saw him.

He was no longer light-headed or dazed. His rash act

seemed completely appropriate. There was muffled laughter from the theater and the sound of Raj's shoes clicking on the bare concrete floor. Another door opened and suddenly Raj faced a large black man in a red coat. He had a cell phone to his ear.

"They didn't tell me nothing about double cheese, but hand-tossed, yeah," he said. When he saw Raj, the man put his hand over the phone.

"This is backstage, man. You want to find your seat the way you came," he said.

"No, I'm a doctor. I have a pass," said Raj. He fished for his emergency medical ID, the one issued when interns do a rotation in an ambulance.

The guard nodded blankly, talking into the phone. "No, this ain't for pickup, it's a delivery."

Raj pulled out the ID and flashed it. His instincts told him to keep walking and not give the guard time to think about why a doctor would be carrying cellophane-wrapped roses. It took him several minutes to find the right door. When he knocked, no one answered. Raj tested the doorknob. Unlocked.

Why was he here? Was it a karmic conspiracy, some unknown force, or merely an attack of infatuation? Love is always called a mystery, but not infatuation. It's the shallow passion, the fling that ends in regret more often than a lasting bond. But what is more mysterious than the sudden flash of desire? Especially if that desire is so secret that you hardly recognize its image in the mirror? Infatuation is hope reborn.

Another surge of loud laughter and applause came from far away. Raj had the feeling that he was going to break someone's heart after all.

2.

LOVE IS WISE enough to make us jump off a cliff when that is the only way to be free. As he barged into Molly's dressing room, Raj's head was filled with pleas to explain what he was doing.

I had to see you because I haven't been able to think about anything else since . . . He couldn't say that, it wasn't honest.

I know I shouldn't be here, but I only need five minutes of your time. What was he, a time-share salesman?

If you feel about me the way I feel about you, you'll know why I'm here. Better.

But he had walked into an empty dressing room. This was the last thing Raj expected, and he almost called out Molly's name, but instead he took a look around. The room wasn't much bigger than a jail cell, with concrete floors and a metal locker against one wall. Molly had surrounded herself with small memorabilia—family pictures, an Off-Broadway poster, satin ballet slippers hanging on a wall. Raj walked over and scanned the pictures for potential lovers or a husband—it hit him that he didn't even know if Molly was married. But she wouldn't keep wedding pictures in this cramped space away from home.

Raj sat down in front of the makeup mirror that tilted on a battered table. He saw someone who looked pale and desperate. There are times when it seems incredibly unfair that the inner man with all his yearning and ideals doesn't show through. Raj turned away so that he didn't have to look. It took half a second to realize that Molly was facing him from the open door.

"How did you get in here?" she asked, her face giving away nothing.

"I had to come, because—"

"Wait, is something wrong? I just have a minute before I go back."

Raj jumped to his feet. "No, not at all. This must seem weird. I was in the audience."

"Okay." Molly continued to stand her ground, holding back the first signs of alarm.

"Well, really, I planned to be in the audience in order to see you again. We didn't even exchange numbers," Raj said. His voice sounded high and rushed. He forced himself to slow down. He didn't step toward her for fear that she might bolt.

Molly let the pause hang there for a second, enough so that Raj could see that his worst fears were false. "It's okay, I was just surprised. It's kind of amazing that you found me," Molly said. She came into the room and smiled.

Raj hadn't come close to revealing his true feelings, but even so, he felt wobbly, so relieved was he that she didn't take him for some intruder. When she got close enough, he took the plunge and opened his arms. Molly hugged him without hesitation. She drew back, and he realized from the slight daze in her eyes that she was still thrilled from the applause and cheers she had just come away from.

"I hate to be frantic," she said breathlessly. "I only ran back here to fix myself up." She sat down at the dressing table and began to dab at her face with makeup. "But you'll stay until the end, won't you?"

"Here?" said Raj, anxious that she might expect him to leave the room.

"You'll miss the rest of the play, but yes, if you want to. Did you bring your Maya? See, I have a good memory." With a guilty start, Raj recalled that he had told Molly of Maya's name.

Still buzzing, Molly got up and moved toward the door, gathering her costume so that the long skirts wouldn't hit the dirty floor.

"No," Raj said. "I'm alone."

Something made Molly pause. She turned and for the first time actually saw him. "Why are you here, exactly? I'm not shocked, but I am amazed."

"I think I'm in love," said Raj.

"With me?"

Raj couldn't answer, and Molly put her hand to her mouth to stop her words a second too late. "How do you know?" she said.

"Know? I didn't put myself on the couch to find out. I'm just here." At a loss for what to do next, Raj stuck the roses out in her direction. Molly stared at them for a second as if they had landed from an alien world.

"Isn't this kind of crazy? I thought you were a psychiatrist," she said.

Raj released a burst of nervous laughter. "I was afraid you were crazy when I first laid eyes on you. A bride jilted at the altar who couldn't let go. Obsessed, wandering the city on a wedding day that never ended."

"Or never began. How Gothic of you," said Molly, not hiding the first signs of displeasure.

Raj held the flowers out again. "Please, just accept them. Please."

Molly took the roses and placed them on the table. "I'm overwhelmed," she said. "A little scared and overwhelmed, to be honest. But I don't have time to be either right now. I have to go." To prove her words, there was another surge of sound from the stage. It triggered Molly into action, and she disappeared before Raj could react.

He stood there paralyzed. His wild romantic gesture had succeeded, but at the same time the results were totally unsatisfactory. How did she feel about him? What could she feel? He was probably lucky that their encounter had been hit and run, because Raj was ready to blurt out words about forces that were larger than both of them. The way he had been brought up, lovers often romanticized that karma brought them together. Daddy-ji and Amma would have said something like that. It was part of the atmosphere of India. But to Molly that might be the same as telling her that she had no choice in the matter.

Raj's excitement was ebbing, and he wondered if fate in this case didn't owe a lot to other things. Loneliness. A girl's beauty. His monkish grind at work. Hormones. The list cooled his blood. There were quite a few ingredients to consider in real life before he threw himself at the gods of karma.

When Raj stole a glance in the mirror, the pale and confused stranger hadn't gone away. He needed to get back in control. But that was a trap, too, because if he opened the window to reason, Maya reappeared. What had he done to her? At the very least he'd betrayed a wonderful person who loved him unconditionally.

A stranger's voice shattered the spell. "Am I interrupting something? The door was open."

A tall, good-looking man entered the room. "I've never seen you before. Are you a friend of Molly's? I am. Does she know you're here, or did you bribe someone?"

The stranger seemed to be in command, and his attitude was grating enough to bring Raj back around. "She asked me to wait here," he said. "But you can wait, too."

The stranger smiled, obeying some code of conduct that forced him to be suave. "Glad to have your permission," he murmured, throwing his coat over a chair but not sitting down. Raj wondered how many people in Molly's world acted and sounded like this. It made him realize how much an intruder he actually was. The stranger spent a moment leafing through a playbill on the table; he poured water from a pitcher and waited.

"Bradley!"

Both men looked startled. Molly came in and threw her arms around the stranger. Raj hadn't counted on the possibility that the act would be over in a few minutes instead of half an hour.

"Why didn't you warn me you were about to give your greatest performance?" the stranger said, looking pleased. "Be a liar and say that it was because you saw me in the fourth row." All the blood ran from Raj's face.

"I'll leave the lying to you," said Molly, lingering in the man's arms. "You're so good at it." The two seemed on terms of undisguised intimacy; Raj didn't need a map. He would have slunk out, but Molly took the tall man's arm and turned him to face Raj. As she introduced them, her voice remained bright and vivacious.

She's still in her dazzle, Raj thought. He stuck his hand out and Bradley shook it loosely.

"I thought we were going out," Bradley said.

"We are. Raj just came by on the spur of the moment," Molly said.

"No doubt. He wouldn't be the first, would he?" It was a bad moment until something caught Raj's eye and saved him. Molly's face was red. Beneath her brightness, she was feeling barely under control.

"He's a new friend," she said quickly. "We catch weddings together." When she noticed that she was being watched, Molly reddened even more, in a fast scarlet flush that began at her neck and swept away any attempt to appear calm. She rushed over to her mirror.

"I haven't even had a chance to wipe this gunk off. So get out, both of you. Five minutes." She picked up her cloths and creams and began working furiously.

"Well, we have our orders," laughed Bradley, pulling Raj away. They emerged from the dressing room into a small gaggle of fans hanging around the door. Raj felt hollow. He looked up at Bradley's handsome, pleased face, which was scanning the hallway for friends.

"She is very good, isn't she?" Bradley said. He directed this remark to the air, as if it belonged to whoever was lucky enough to catch it. Raj heard a soft click behind him. He turned and saw the dressing room door open a crack. A pale sliver of Molly's face appeared in it. "Come back here," she whispered. The crack opened wider, and he slipped in.

Molly shut the door and moved away from him, pacing back and forth while still wiping makeup from her face. "What's happening?" she said. She began to cry, the tears dragging pink streaks down her rouged cheeks.

"Maybe you're feeling something," Raj said. "It's okay. Run the spool backwards. It's ten minutes ago, and you're glad to see me and I'm thrilled to find that it was you in the newspaper after I almost lost you. Please understand, I'm a normal person. At least I was normal. This wasn't something planned. I didn't mean to barge in when your fiancé wanted to be alone with you."

"Lord," Molly said. "I don't believe you." Then with the only irrationality that makes life worth living, she kissed him. It wasn't the longest or deepest kiss Raj had ever experienced. Her warm hands and the slight awkward lurch of her body as she hastily approached him made more of an impression. But what he was looking for was there—the hint that Molly might be meant for him, and that she might want to be with him.

"There," she said, drawing back. She said it like someone who has put the finishing touch on a painting or paid the last installment on a bill. "We're both too impulsive for our own good, so we can start with that. I hope you don't turn out to be a disaster. And he's not my fiancé."

Raj could see that the kiss had calmed her down. When a sharp rap came at the door and Bradley stuck his head back in, Molly looked cheerful and self-possessed again. After waiting patiently, six fans came in. A couple were acting students, two girls from the same TriBeCa loft class that Molly had taken three years before, as it turned out. Praise gushed as freely as tap water. *Wonderful, marvelous, darling, divine.* Raj didn't have command of those words, had never heard them tossed around as common coinage except on television. Molly was patient and gracious. She talked with each person attentively, only occasionally letting her glance drift back to Raj.

"Have you known her long?" Raj asked Bradley, who had produced a re-corked bottle of wine from somewhere.

"Eight years. Hand me a couple of those plastic cups over there," Bradley said. "Make it three. I assume you're staying." Raj found the cups and held them out for Bradley to pour.

"I don't know about that," said Raj.

"Oh, you have to," Bradley said. "You're smitten, right? It's demanded of the smitten." He could have been putting Raj in his place, but there was an amused compassion in his voice.

Raj looked at his watch and panicked. "I have to go now. But I'll try to come back. If she can wait, tell Molly that I'll be at the back door."

Before Bradley could react, Raj ran out of the room while Molly had her back to him. He raced down the dark corridors past the guard. Maya was waiting for him in the deserted lobby.

She said, "Have you been looking for me? I thought you said the Broadway side. What's wrong?"

"Nothing. Just a mixup. I have to get back to the hospital, but I talked them into postponing my shift until I could meet you. What time is it now?"

"Ten-thirty," said Maya.

"That's not so bad. I promised them eleven. Are you okay going home by yourself?" Raj knew that Maya wouldn't object. As she kissed him, his mind was already plotting the shortest path to the back door. No guilt, no pangs about lying ever entered his mind. Even after Maya was safely in a cab and he was running to find Molly, Raj didn't think of it as cheating. Passion isn't a thinking animal.

Bradley and Molly were waiting for him outside the stage door. She said, "I know it's late, but I'm dying to eat a Reuben sandwich. Anyone else hungry?"

"I prefer not to mix pastrami and fine wine," said Bradley, raising the paper cup he still had in his hand. Left alone with Raj, Molly said, "Let's walk now. You need air." In the heavy summer humidity that was just beading up on windows of shops and cafés, they headed toward the all-night delis on Eighth Avenue. It was a while before either said anything more.

"You're kind of perfect right now," Molly murmured. "If I never got to find out one more thing about you, it would all be much safer. By perfect I mean you're the perfect stranger, the way you simply lost control and wanted to sweep me away."

"I'm not getting a good feeling about the next part," said Raj.

Molly smiled. "I don't know what kind of fantasy you rode in on. Maybe you feel like ditching now. You can tell me."

"No, definitely not," Raj said firmly.

"Come here," Molly said. She reached up and touched his cheek.

"It's a very rare person who would do what you just did," she said delicately. "I'm not closed off. I understand what it took. But maybe I should worry."

"I didn't set out to hurt anyone. That's not my intention," Raj said. "I can't explain why I adore you."

Molly laughed with pleased embarrassment. "You sound like a kid who owns my calendar."

Raj couldn't deny it. But melting at her feet wouldn't get him much further than this evening. Molly read his mind. "If you stay just the way you are this minute, we won't last two weeks, but where can this go?" she said.

"I didn't bring a map. We'll just have to find out," said Raj.

Molly took his arm with a sigh. "Maps are a waste," she said. *"Listen, act, feel.* That's how to find your way." The sidewalks still radiated the day's heat, and the damp air carried ugly smells wafting from the alleys, but Raj felt the happy exhaustion of victory.

When they got to the place with the good pastrami, Raj was too tired to eat. "Can I just watch you?" he asked. The abject simplicity of his plea caught Molly off guard. "You have so much faith in me. Maybe I'm going to find out that you get a dozen girls that way."

"No, just don't make too much fun of me."

She said, "All right, you can sit there and watch me eat pickles, but then you need to decompress, and I'm a little tired and nervous. I need to soak my feet and think. Can we try again in a couple of days?" Raj reluctantly nodded.

"Don't look so worried," Molly said. "My answer might be yes."

RAJ FOUND HIMSELF in a new reality, bewildered, excited, and apprehensive. He continued his relationship with Maya. They had dinner as often as their schedules allowed; she slept over when Raj pulled a day off twice a month. But his life and Molly's also became intertwined. She never referred to Maya after that first night, and she made sure to tell Raj well in advance what nights the theater was dark. Most of the time nothing meshed, and they stole most of their hours in the afternoon.

"I ask myself why we're together," she said one Sunday stretched out on a park bench. "What made me go with you out of the subway? I was going to miss the wedding anyway."

"Impulse," Raj suggested. "You said so yourself."

"That's the American version," Molly replied. "Something's going on here, and we both want to find out what it is. I don't want to rush into words like love. Not yet, and not too fast."

"I agree," Raj said, going along. "Besides, when someone says 'I love you' the other person usually says it right back, almost automatically. It loses something."

"I know," Molly said, "it should mean something."

"What kind of word do you want, then?" asked Raj.

"The one you find at the very instant you don't have to say it."

"Ah, a mystery," said Raj. "I like that." Smiling, he wondered if he really did.

The first time she came to his apartment, Molly peeked into the refrigerator while he put on some jazz in the living/dining room.

"What's this?" she said, peering at the top shelves. "It's like a little army." The fridge was lined with small plastic tubs, each covered in foil, lined up in neat ranks and files.

"Food for a week," Raj said. "Spaghetti marinara, cole slaw, and instant banana pudding."

She wrinkled her nose. "So basically you subsist on cold cabbage, soggy pasta, and artificially flavored goop."

Raj came around behind her and closed the refrigerator door. "I'm organized. It's a must at this stage, and the time I save cooking or going out gives me more time to read journals and get some rest." He was irked that she didn't understand how much pressure he lived under. "The first week I interned, I was put in charge of the night shift at a cardiac ward in the veteran's hospital, a huge monster of a place in Queens, which means eighty patients with damaged hearts whose life or death might depend on me. I was also expected to update charts and cover the emergency room from midnight to six. In the first four hours I saw two heart attacks, a bleeding ulcer, a woman in diabetic shock who could go into a coma at any moment, and a man who had either cut himself shaving or tried to commit suicide. Not a lot of men decide to shave at two in the morning. No one died on my shift, which was some kind of miracle, and all I could think about as I fell onto my narrow metal cot in some dark converted closet set aside for interns was one thing: *Yesterday I was just a student.* It blows your mind to have so much responsibility thrust at you without warning, and it scares the crap out of you."

She looked impressed. Taking her home afterward, Raj kissed her gently and said, "This is very different from anything else I've ever been through. I feel like I'm watching myself. As if another person is walking and talking. It's strange."

Another woman might have interpreted this as pulling away, but Molly instantly caught on. "I know exactly. That's my living. I go on stage feeling that way every night. I watch *her,* and she's so good. So confident. I sometimes wish I could let her do it all."

"Would she be playing a part right now?" asked Raj.

"That's not what I mean. When you can look down and see yourself, you know it's just a role. Most people don't. They get so caught up in their part that they think it's real. But once you can watch yourself, then it's like being free, isn't it?" Molly hadn't talked this way before, although Raj had heard her refer to her onstage persona as *she.* It was *she* who gave off lilac-scented air in the play and moved with rehearsed grace. Molly herself was apart and different; she had to be learned separately from what you saw.

Standing on Molly's doorstep, Raj felt impelled to tell her about one of his family's strangest episodes. Daddy-ji had an older brother named Girish. Nobody talked about him, and when they did, the tone was somber, the way you'd talk about the dead. When Raj was fifteen, Daddy-ji rushed back to India because his mother was gravely ill. The illness could have been fatal, but it passed, and when Daddy-ji returned home, the first thing he did was to take a picture of Girish from his suitcase and place it on the mantel where all the other portraits stood.

Amma was quite surprised at this restoration to respectability. "The boy is old enough to hear everything," Daddy-ji said. The three of them sat on cushions before the family shrine. "My brother was lost to us, but you don't know why," he told Raj. "Now you will." Girish, it turned out, had been a soldier wounded out after some heavy skirmishes in Kashmir. During his convalescence, he was placed next to a Muslim sergeant in the hospital; this man served in the Indian army and had been caught by mortar fire in the same region. The two became friends, and when they were discharged, they became neighbors in a suburb of Jabalpur, near the military cantonment.

"This sergeant had a beautiful wife," said Daddy-ji. "Girish took no notice of her. She brought out mint tea or kabobs, then she disappeared. It's the custom, and if my brother saw her twice without her veil, I wouldn't believe it. Only one day I got a telegram, and he had run away with her. Just like that. The husband went into a rage, and then cried for three months. For a long time no one heard from the runaways until my brother showed up in Poona to cash a paycheck. And even then he had nothing to say, except that they were together."

"When did this happen?" asked Raj.

"You were lucky. You weren't born yet," said Daddy-ji.

The scandal ripped the family apart. The two brothers stopped speaking, and for all intents and purposes Girish ceased to exist for two decades. Until their mother seemed to be on her deathbed, when Girish was afraid that he might never see Daddy-ji again.

"One night my brother caught me by surprise, waiting under the portico at your grandmother's house. I tried to throw him off, but he held me tight, with a soldier's grip. He had suffered a long time in silence."

The tale that poured out was very strange. It began when Yasmin, the sergeant's wife, showed up unannounced at Girish's door. Although she was behind the veil, he felt nervous letting her in. She pleaded with him, however, and he reluctantly stepped aside. Ignoring all the rules of purdah, Yasmin bared her shoulder. "See this?" she said. Then she showed him her right arm. In both places there was a small red sore, no larger than a pimple.

"They are so painful," Yasmin lamented.

Girish was sweating now. He asked his neighbor's wife what the sores had to do with him, and Yasmin explained that she had had a dream. "I dreamed that you touched them and they went away. These sores are everywhere on my body. I am in agony," she said, breaking down in tears. There was nothing to do. She wouldn't go away, and even though Girish thought she must be either crazy or demonized, he touched her shoulder and right arm.

"How strange," Amma said, although she seemed to understand something that Raj couldn't grasp.

"More than strange," said Daddy-ji. "The next day this Yasmin came back, overjoyed. Every sore on her body was miraculously healed. She dropped her clothes in front of Girish, and every inch of skin was pure and fresh. The next day they ran off together, leaving the sergeant to his rage and his tears."

Since Girish's confession only made the elopement more scandalous, Raj didn't understand why he was suddenly back in favor. It was some years before Daddy-ji told him the rest. "My brother isn't a superstitious man, but when he saw Yasmin's naked body, he fell in love. Not with the woman but with her soul. He was overwhelmed with belief that two souls can come together for a miracle, so he had no choice but to accept his fate and run away with her."

The upshot was that this miracle was something Raj's family could accept. It brought his uncle back among the living.

"Why did you remember this now?" asked Molly.

"Because Girish only began to love Yasmin when he saw outside himself. He must have had that feeling we just talked about, when you look down and you aren't the part you're playing. He was above and beyond, the way Yasmin had dreamed about him."

Molly found it a strange and beautiful story. "We should all dream about each other that way—every love should begin with a touch that you have to have." Because he felt that way about her, Raj looked back on this as the moment when they began to merge.

The tale came up again a few days later. "I think your father left something out," Molly said. "Didn't Girish want to sleep with Yasmin when she showed him her body?"

"I imagine he couldn't keep his hands off of her." Raj laughed. "That would be the American version."

Soon after that, he saw Molly naked for the first time. It didn't happen on the refrigerator night. A week later, he led her down the narrow, murky brown hallway that he hadn't bothered to repaint. His bedroom had crimped blinds that barely kept out the neon Bud Light sign from the bar across the street. They were both tired but exhilarated after seeing a movie they had both loved.

He didn't say, "You're sure?" She didn't tell him what to do to please her. They let laughter and affection carry them across the thorny part, meaning the decision to take this step, and without saying so, they agreed that sex didn't mean any promises. Raj was tremendously relieved that Molly showed any passion for him. She stood by the bed and slowly took off every piece of clothing as deliberately as if she had to keep her school uniform neat for the next morning, and as she laid out her skirt on the only chair in the room, she laughed softly.

"What is it?" he asked, already undressed and sitting

on the bed waiting for her, enjoying the slowness of her ritual.

"A man should never see a woman take off pantyhose. It's the least sexy thing next to taking off hiking boots."

"This man doesn't mind."

Raj reached out and asked for her hand with his. She accepted and came closer. A muscle in her cheek quivered as he kissed her, and he realized that her nervous remark hadn't been a way of keeping distant from him or reminding herself that this was an intimacy she wanted to have. Molly was just not that experienced, and she found herself in a strange bedroom.

He was careful to be attentive and slow, and when the time came to forget everything and lose himself in their warm entwining, they both did. It thrilled him to finally feel her bring herself to him physically, as he hoped she did with their first kiss.

But a little time afterward, when he reached over to caress her again, Molly moved away and, in a voice that bothered him with its calmness, said she had to go.

"Why?" he asked. "We both came, didn't we?"

"Don't," she half-whispered. Molly looked pained; it was really the first thing he had ever said that disappointed her. He wanted to apologize, but once Molly was out of bed she became cheerful and affectionate again, leaning low across the sheets to kiss him as she slipped on her top. She asked him not to walk her to the subway, though, and as she closed the door Raj felt the air grow more pensive. But the room wasn't empty. Molly was still there without being there. Raj wondered if it was the same for her. Would he be with Molly when she walked into her empty apartment?

3.

THE NEXT MORNING after Molly left, the phone rang. Raj wasn't up yet—it was six o'clock—but he was awake with his own thoughts. He picked it up and said softly, "Do you know how wonderful this has been?"

"Raj?" The voice at the other end was Maya's. Words stuck in his throat; his heart pounded so hard that he heard it in his ears.

Finally he mumbled, "Did I say something strange? I was asleep."

There was a pause. When Maya spoke again she sounded upset. "My parents had to rush back to India last night. One of my grandparents has been in a car accident, and he might not live."

It was Baba, the grandfather that was closest to her, who had given her toys that she still kept in a special drawer. "I'll be right over," said Raj.

Maya opened the door in her bathrobe. She looked pale but was trying not to weep. "I should be over there, but I can't, not with school and my job. Last night I thought I'd be okay about my parents leaving, but now I'm so lonely," she said.

Raj pulled her to the sofa to console her. "Maybe he'll be all right. Don't dwell on the worst."

"No, something isn't right. It's not just Baba, it's you," Maya said hesitantly.

The blood drained from Raj's whole body. "Me? What do you mean?" he said.

"Don't you know?" asked Maya.

"No. I really don't. Tell me." Raj's mind was racing through the hundred words he could throw out to divert Maya's attention, but it was fixed on him.

"You don't seem to want to be with me, and when you are, you're still somewhere else," said Maya, beginning to cry now that she had released what she had been afraid even to admit to herself.

"Don't be ridiculous," said Raj, only to see her look even more wounded.

"This isn't ridiculous," said Maya. "It's very hard for me. I love you."

"I love you, too. We're getting married soon, and this is the kind of doubt that crops up," said Raj. The objectivity in his voice gave him more confidence. "It's very normal to feel like this. It's a way for the unconscious to deal with fears about getting married."

"You think so?" said Maya, wiping her eyes.

Raj held her closer. "Yes, I do. Anxiety and doubt just come up, that's all."

It took some time, but Maya began to feel better. She dabbed the tears away with a tissue; her face was puffy and not made up. "Let me get you something," she said.

"No, sit," said Raj. "I'll fetch you some tea."

He brought her the tea, and after she had drunk half a cup, Maya asked Raj to hold her. She'd stayed up all night and she soon fell asleep against Raj's body. He could feel her heaving chest slowly subside. He was feeling horribly guilty but helpless at the same time. Maya could be blamed for nothing but offering him happiness. So why was he betraying her? If he was put on the stand, Raj couldn't have mounted a coherent defense. He wasn't cheating for adventure or to be understood. It wasn't the thrill of secrecy; he had no grudges against Maya, not even an issue. To say that he didn't love her was a lie; he knew he did.

Raj pointed the remote at the televison and put it on mute. He pretended to watch CNN as guilt continued to gnaw. His frayed nerves made the images a garbled smear. A school bus had tipped off the road in Haiti. Abortion protesters marched in front of the White House. In some hopeless land, terrified children ran down the street fleeing silent bombs and voiceless machine guns.

"I have to go," Raj whispered when he felt Maya stirring again. He left her with the impression that he was going to work. This wasn't true. Raj spent the day away from his apartment, tending to errands. When they were done he went to a movie. He didn't call either Maya or Molly.

It was twilight before Raj got back to his place. He changed quickly and took the bus to Heartbreak House. That was Maya's nickname for the psychiatric floor, and she was right—Raj did work in a house of sorrow. Its official title was the Jacob and Enid Seckler Pavilion. The name made it sound like the place should have cabanas by a pool and an Italian coffee bar. It didn't. A cheerful glassed-in day room and red patterned carpeting can't perform miracles. The minute Raj got off the elevator on the sixth floor, a familiar wave of misery struck him like noxious factory fumes.

A short, bald man was standing there, ready to way-lay anyone coming out of the elevator. "I'm in pain; I need more of that stuff," he complained. Raj recognized him, a long-term depressive who used suicide attempts to get back to the hospital fairly often. He had a good streak of passive aggression.

One of the nurses ran up. "We're all in pain, Mr. Morgenstern. Please get back into line." Meds were doled out twice a day at the nurses' station. Raj could see the lineup forming for the seven o'clock ritual.

Mr. Morgenstern was resisting. "You don't give me what my doctor ordered. I told him I was in pain, and he said I could have more stuff."

"You go ahead. I'll check your chart as soon as I can," said Raj. He followed as Mr. Morgenstern allowed him-self to be led away.

"You're early," said Mona. "It's pretty calm tonight. Can I get you anything?"

"No, but thanks," Raj said. Mona was sitting before her large tray of medications. A good helpful Catholic girl in her twenties, Mona didn't really enjoy the com-pany of psychotics; she felt most useful dispensing their drugs. On the tray was arranged a grid of white paper cups, each filled with a basic minimum of milk of magnesia and Seconal. Patients always had bad digestion, and the sleeping pill was for the staff's benefit as much as theirs. Most cups also contained the psychotropic drugs that were meant to relieve a wide variety of mental anguish.

The patients milling aimlessly around Mona were evenly divided between men and women of all ages. A few formed into pairs of friends; most were as alone as their condition fated them to be.

"That pill is rat poison," one woman muttered, staring into the cup Mona handed her. "I know you've been slipping it to me. It doesn't work. I'm shielded against it. Zoop." She wove a magical gesture around the pill with her free hand.

"Fine, Frances," Mona said. "When the doctor reviews your chart tonight, I'm sure he'll take that into consideration."

She was referring to Raj, who was in charge of the floor as long as he was on call. It was a firm rule that any private patient admitted to the care of the hospital was no longer under a private physician's direct care. They had been turned over to the psych ward, which meant that Raj had more say in their treatment than their original doctor. But in actuality he hardly ever changed meds or wrote new orders on a chart, not unless the patient was having an extreme allergic reaction or had become a danger to himself. In the absence of an emergency, the patients mostly needed a highly trained, empathic, insightful, never bored, and ever involved baby-sitter.

"Hello, Ira, how are you feeling?" Raj asked one of the older men, a rail-thin psychotic who always fought being committed when his family could no longer deal with his episodes.

"Lousy, and I won't get better until someone pays attention to my real doctor, not some beginner like you."

When he wasn't acting out and screaming at strangers in stores, Ira acted very dependent. He deeply resented the fact that Dr. Schiff, a third-year resident who had moved on to the psychoanalytic institute, had left him. He would attack any replacement, no matter how often they assured him that he was in good hands.

"Let me take a look at my schedule, then maybe we can talk this evening," said Raj. "You have a very interesting case." He was applying the magic formula, which never failed.

Ira's narrow face brightened up. "Gimme that," he barked, taking the paper cup held out by Mona. "You can bet the farm that I have an interesting case. I know Dr. Schiff had a lot to say about it." Actually, Norm Schiff had raced off so fast that he left barely a paragraph of off-chart jottings about his patient, but Raj nodded and smiled. "So we'll talk," he said. He cast a benign and interested gaze over the other patients, an automatic reflex that told them he wasn't playing favorites. They all wanted the one commodity more precious than gold: attention.

Raj noticed two other nurses at the station. One was filling out daily reports, preparing for the regular staff conference on Thursdays; the other was reading a romance novel. Both looked up when they heard his voice. Raj rushed on before they could pay much attention to him.

"Don't be a stranger," one called after him.

"He looks pretty good walking away, if you ask me," said the other, a single mother named Joanie who was never one to disguise a hint. Joanie felt that a psych ward should be free of inhibition. Her come-ons made Raj feel flattered and mildly embarrassed, but his head was so filled with Molly that he wasn't going to look back. Joanie had served as a source of comfort for more than one crop of interns. The only thing she had to worry about was somebody tattling in group.

Raj got to his small office and shut the door. Of the two women in his life, the one who came to mind without being summoned was Molly. She came to him now. Reflexively Raj picked up the phone and dialed Maya.

"Any better?" he said. "Is there news on Baba?"

"No. I'm so blue. How was work?" Maya said dully.

"I'm still here. I pulled a double shift," Raj lied.

They exchanged commiserations and he hung up. Whether from guilt or caution, he didn't dial Molly. Even after a few weeks, he didn't have a clear idea how much attention she would accept from him. How strange that the precious commodity every patient craved from Raj might not be welcome, might frighten her off or arouse irritability. In psychiatry, love is an issue because everything is an issue. The other staff psychiatrists, when Raj met them at the next group session on Friday, would be sharp to notice if he showed any change in behavior. If Raj squirmed, his mind wandering from the case at hand, every wriggle would be interpreted around the table, silently or out loud. Raj wouldn't mind if he didn't have anything to hide. He'd already shared a dozen intimate details about Maya. The pavilion was its own peculiar world, one that he had agreed to be in. But that didn't mean he would throw Molly to them next, not while he could keep her protected.

There was a tap at the door, and Habib stuck his head

in. "I saw your name on the duty sheet," he said. "How are you feeling? I've been mulling over that story you told me. About the girl on the subway."

"Who?" said Raj. He forgot that he had told Habib the story of the redhead in the wedding dress when it was still just that—a story.

"You should let me see her. I'm open. Actually, I'm starved," said Habib. "She's an actress, right?"

"I don't think your schedules would match too well," said Raj. Habib was a first-year resident, one year ahead of Raj, a well-born Saudi who had been trained at Tufts and then served his internship at Beth Israel, one of Boston's temples of medicine. He was flip but very astute.

"The only people who have matching schedules with us have already gone to hell," said Habib cheerfully.

"It wouldn't work," said Raj.

Habib gave him a sharp look. "Am I missing something here?" he said. While in training, a shrink is expected to treat the rest of the psychiatric staff like family. This kind of forced sharing is meant to develop trust and honesty. At the moment Raj didn't feel all that trusting.

"There's nothing to confide," Raj said, carefully measuring his evasion. "I don't have her number."

"You could have said that from the beginning."

"I was letting you down gently." Raj tried to make it sound like a joke.

"Actually, I wish you two were getting it on," said Habib. "All women, but especially new ones, will bring your shit up fast. You'd spill so much in group that I wouldn't have to participate. Which is fine with me. I'll hold the Kleenex."

Raj went back to his charts. Even if Habib wasn't fooled, he could be counted on to be discreet. Or was he fooling Raj?

"How much is Meeker on right now?" Raj asked, riffling through some notes in front of him. "He's agitated and unresponsive. I think he's speaking in tongues again when the staff isn't around." For certain patients either too much or too little medication causes restless, chaotic behavior, the exact opposite of what the drugs should do, especially in the unpredictable swings of schizophrenia.

"I forget. It's in there," said Habib. "The attending's notes are a mess. So have fun. I'm gonna crash."

As the door closed, Raj knew they had been doing a little dance. Raj was expected to sound cool, in control no matter how much turmoil he might be experiencing in his personal life. Habib was expected to sound open but unintrusive. Anything Raj wanted to divulge would fall on sympathetic ears, then instantly get passed along to the other residents and to Clarence. Molly being an actress must have piqued their curiosity already. Raj could imagine their comments.

Maybe he can't handle emotion.

Which is why he needs a woman to act them out on.

Or overplay them.

Possible hysteric.

Good point.

A strange little dance indeed. Five hours passed with a slowness that could set records. Raj kept his head down in the pile of charts, but he felt his pent-up longing swelling. Images of being in bed with Molly dominated his thoughts. He was at that stage where she held the key to his greatest joy and greatest misery. He woke up that morning aware of this, but now the feeling came back stronger, and reverberated throughout his body. When the clock was decently past midnight but not yet one o'clock, he picked up the phone and dialed.

"Hello?" a groggy voice answered.

"Hi, it's me. Are you asleep?"

"That's the rumor." Molly didn't sound too put out. Her performance usually got her home around midnight; she was used to falling asleep close to one.

"About last night. I'm constantly reliving it," said

Raj. There was a pause at the other end that lasted long enough to stop his heart.

"Let me turn down the TV, okay?" said Molly. The television in the background didn't sound that loud, and Raj worried that she was buying time. When she came back, Molly said, "I was thinking about it, too. I almost stepped on Guy's line tonight." Guy's existence still irritated Raj. He was neither gay nor on drugs, or anything comforting like that. "I kept thinking how sweet you were."

"Really?" Raj said, hoping for more. There was another silence, then he said, "I'm sorry to bother you. I know how late it is and how tired you are, but I wanted to hear your voice."

"Good thing, too. I was planning to dematerialize right after Letterman is over."

"You aren't supposed to make fun of me too much, remember?" said Raj.

"Yes. And I won't. I want to relive last night, too. There are a few details that slipped my mind," said Molly. "I think a refresher would be good for both of us."

"Absolutely. I love you, now get your sleep. I'll call when I'm released from here."

"That will be nice."

The phone clicked, and happy as he was, Raj felt a

small twinge. Tonight he would like to have heard "I love you, too" in return. He got up and began doing some stretching exercises.

The tiny office was still closing in, so he went out. The hall was deserted, but as he passed by each room, Raj heard all the night sounds of a ward—ragged coughs and snoring, the groans of troubled sleep, whisperings between two old ladies who had found kinship in insomnia, the faint babbling of a paranoid who read the Bible relentlessly until irresistible fatigue forced his eyes closed.

Mona spotted him and came down the hall, meeting Raj halfway to the nurses' station. "Joanie had a bad date last night. Would you believe that you can waste a whole evening on a guy and he still doesn't put out?" Mona laughed and pulled Raj toward the day room. It was empty, and they sank into two armchairs pulled up beside the TV.

"Joanie's not interested, is she? I mean in me?" asked Raj.

"I could tell you, but if I save it for group, she'll be there, too. That would be more honest, wouldn't it?"

Raj smiled crookedly. He was glad Mona had a sense of irony about the whole family business. "I'm in love," he said. "I haven't told any of the others."

"Her name's Maya?" asked Mona.

"This is another one."

Mona took the news calmly. "Are you drawing me into furtive intimacy by sharing this personal fact?" she asked. "We might be violating our contract with the group."

"Cut it out," said Raj. "It's for real."

Mona's expression softened. "You have a crush on someone who's not medicated? That's great. Really."

"Thanks, but it's driving me crazy. I threw myself at this girl like a mortar shell, and it's amazing she didn't call the police. Now she wants to be close to me, I can tell, but what's next?"

"Are you asking because you smell danger?" Mona asked.

"Is being out of your depth dangerous?" Raj asked.

"Sure. But I think that's the whole point. Unless you just want to play around." Mona said all this quickly, knowing what she was talking about. Then she hesitated.

"What?" asked Raj.

"You got through to her with an emotional ambush. Some women can take that, but it puts too much on the man. She's got to carry her share of approaching you with needs or complaints or just private stuff. It's inevitable. You can't detour fears. Defenses don't stay down forever."

Raj listened carefully. He wasn't surprised to hear

such wise opinions from Mona; all the nurses had gone through special psychiatric training. But Mona was one of the few who had started out with a basic sense of how people work in their secret places. It was a gift, and Raj wasn't sure he had it yet. That's what made him confide in Mona above anyone else.

"Do you usually hurl yourself at women? I mean, is that your tactic of choice?" asked Mona.

"Not at all. I've never done anything like that before. Christ, can you believe I was actually on a date with Maya, and I ran backstage just to get close to this woman. Molly. That's her name. I bought roses. I fondled the street clothes draped over her chair. If you talk about this in group, I'll kill you."

"Wow." Mona looked at him a certain way. "That was really kind of a bastard thing to do—to your date."

"She doesn't know. I was careful," said Raj quickly, feeling the wave of disapproval that was coming toward him. "I feel guilty all the time now."

"But not enough to tell her?"

"No."

"At least you sound mournful," said Mona. A new, skeptical tone had crept into her voice. Mona could be brutally direct with patients who got out of control, and Raj was not so high up on the ladder that she had to pull her punches. "I would feel a lot better discussing this in group. Sorry. I'll be more glad for you after we talk this through," she said.

When she got up and left, Raj was alarmed. He thought he could pour his heart out to Mona, and now it had backfired. He might be humiliated in group. A lot of blood was shed around the table in the name of trying to get to real emotions. Mona's disapproval wasn't a good sign. She and Habib had turned into his allies. They buffered each other when the inquisition got too close. Not that that couldn't change. Whatever happened in group, however, Raj promised himself to make this all up to Maya.

He had a lot on his mind when he looked up and saw a patient, Mrs. Klemper, coming toward him in her bathrobe. She had a wicked gleam in her eye. "You're up very late," Raj said, trying to restore his calm. "Having trouble sleeping? We might have the nurses give you something."

Mrs. Klemper snorted and waved her hand as carelessly as a rhino brushes off a gnat. "What do I need with a pill? You want to avoid me. You think I can't read a face like the sorry one you're wearing?"

Raj felt his heart sink. Officially, although he was the doctor on call that night, he stood very low on the staff totem pole. Most of the patients didn't recognize that. To them, every doctor was an authority, the only exception being "my" doctor, whose rank was higher than anyone else's. But a few were observant enough to see who was green and needed their noses rubbed in it. Mr. Morgenstern, the bellyaching passive aggressor, wasn't even the most vocal or the nastiest.

That honor belonged to Claudia—Mrs. Klemper—a fiftyish woman from Brooklyn who had been in and out of the hospital five times since Raj joined the service that summer. She came through the revolving door whenever her husband had an affair. Since Mr. Klemper, who traveled a lot, sustained a regular appetite for casual sex, or so Claudia wailed during one of her crashes, she had a constant source of complaint. Forever the victim, she never asked why she had picked a rover like Mr. Klemper, or why his totally predictable forays into flesh so devastated her.

It seemed only natural to her that she should act out her anger on the floor. A week ago, for example, she broke into the pantry and began hurling cans of soup, coffee, mixed nuts, and evaporated milk in all directions. Her disheveled dress exposed half her bosom and her hair flew out in gray, scraggly wisps as she shouted, "You don't know a damn thing about me!" to Raj, whose patient she was.

It took a lot to calm Claudia down during that tantrum. "Why the hell did they send you, a kid?" she screamed. "Real doctors are idiots, but they are Einsteins compared to you. Got that?"

Now Claudia was fuming again, and although any man would do, Raj guessed that he'd won the lottery. She would burn him for neglecting to call on her earlier that evening. Raj searched his mind for something to say. Claudia was the only patient who had responded—after he said, "You have a very interesting case"—with a cynical smile and the words, "That tired old shit? You could try being a little less typical, you know."

Claudia broke the silence first. "You look sad, kid. Somebody chew your ass?"

"I'm not sad, Claudia."

"Suit yourself."

"Perhaps it's you who's feeling sad. Is that why you are still up?" said Raj. This reply didn't make him feel very bright, but at least he was obeying rule number one in therapy: *Never share personal information about yourself with a patient.*

"Sad? What gave you that impression—the fact that my marriage is falling apart and if he leaves me I have nobody? I would be doing cartwheels if only it wouldn't fracture my hip."

"I know you have genuine reasons to be sad. It's okay; this is a safe place. You don't have to push the topic away by making fun of it," said Raj, thinking that at least he was beginning to sound professional. Mrs. Klemper looked slightly less hostile. Raj could sense it, and he had been waiting a long time for her to open up even slightly, to expose a bit of the massive fear lurking behind her hostile mask. He patted her hand. "I'd like to hear whatever you want to share," he told her.

"Really?" said Mrs. Klemper.

"Yes. It's quiet here and we're alone. What would you like to say?"

"Well," she said, thinking. "First off, I'd like to share that if I had any guts, I would take a butcher knife and turn my husband from a bull to a steer. And secondly, I don't know which is more pathetic, your attempts to get me to confide in you or the ridiculous face you're wearing."

Mrs. Klemper shot him a triumphant grin and got up. As she padded toward her room in her fuzzy slippers, Raj supposed she would probably sleep very well for the rest of the night. When he related the incident at group, he could be sure that someone would point out that he shouldn't invest too much in the fantasy that he could help everyone. There are no magic bullets in healing the human mind when it doesn't want to be healed.

4.

RAJ DECIDED TO take on more night shifts so that he could have dinner with Molly before she went to the theater. He found himself barely thinking of Maya; he frequently made excuses when she wanted to see him. He and Molly had discovered a bistro halfway between Broadway and the hospital. One evening Bradley showed up with her.

"Table for three tonight?" the headwaiter asked. He was used to seeing them as a couple. Raj nodded and followed him to a cramped table near the swinging doors to the kitchen. Bradley was breezy and nonchalant, making Raj wonder if this was his only mood.

"She seduced me with paella. This city is a desert for Spanish food, but she says this place is *muy bueno.*"

"You're upset, I can tell," Molly said.

"No, I'm glad we're all here," Raj lied. He buried his face in the menu while she turned her attention back to Bradley and the details of Catalan cooking. Not that Bradley was a stranger anymore. Raj knew that he had met Molly in summer stock when he was toying with the idea of becoming a director. Now he was stuck in the family's brokerage house. Raj realized that he had to make room for other people in her life. Molly wasn't going to hand him a parcel of memories and say, "Here, burn these."

Halfway through dinner he realized that he couldn't take it. "I'm in hell. Bradley, I want to be alone with Molly. I live for these moments, and usually I can barely see her for half an hour before my shifts start."

Bradley's composure was flustered—at first—but before he could answer, Raj continued his outburst. "It makes me crazy that you've been close to her so much longer than I have, and I hope to God Molly admires me someday as much as she admires you. Would you mind leaving us?"

The other two stared at him. Then Molly put down her napkin and stood up. "Excuse me, I have to find the ladies'," she said. She turned to Bradley. "You stay, hear me?"

Bradley held up the wine bottle in Raj's direction. "Well said, my friend. Another glass?" he asked.

"No," said Raj glumly. "Now I've screwed up big time. You should stay. I'm sorry."

"Why? It's fairly clear to all of us that if Molly walked on water you'd be kneeling on the other side with a towel to dry her feet. May I?" Bradley poured himself a glass and sat back. "Has she told you about us?"

"Not really."

"We go back a long way, as you know. She's always been there, ever since she got out of college in Wisconsin and came to New York, where life begins. She helped me through a nasty breakup involving a true love who turned out to have certain financial gains in the back of her mind. My worst Christmas ever, to say the least. I helped Molly through a pregnancy scare three years ago. Her worst spring ever. It was a false alarm. Molly trusts you more than almost anyone I've seen her with. Oh, and we've never been to bed."

Bradley said everything with a briskness suitable for outlining a client's portfolio assets.

"Oh." Raj hadn't expected any kind of divulgence.

He had no fantasies that Molly had never slept with anyone else, but still he was mortified to hear the words "pregnancy scare," and he had to fight off images of her in bed with someone else.

"She's not so strange, although she may act it," Bradley went on. "Molly is special, and she lives by a code. Only she isn't going to tell you that code."

"Has she told you?"

Bradley shook his head. "Not as such. Some people you learn about from what they tell you, but she's the kind who reveals by what she leaves out. I've never heard her say, 'I'm worth it.' She's never dismissed me with 'Whatever.' She doesn't swear, even though her parents do—I've heard them—and the surest sign that she might be in love is that it's the one word she will avoid like the plague."

"Why? I don't understand. Does she want me to suffer?" Desperation won over pride and Raj found himself looking at Bradley as his confidant.

"It's not you. It's the code. I think there's too much love there to talk about."

"So if I lived by the same code, we'd spend our days never saying how we felt. It makes no sense," Raj grumbled. "I can't read her mind. Am I supposed to pass some kind of test?"

"Men are always passing tests. We do it in our sleep.

We do it even when no one has set them." Bradley emptied his wine, and for a second Raj felt a small wave of admiration. Savoir faire was not his cup of tea, but this man was not as slight as he tried to make others believe.

Molly seemed somber when she returned, and there was no more chitchat about Spanish food as they ate in silence. Clearly she sensed that they had discussed her. When the check came and Raj stood up, she told Bradley, "I want to walk Raj to the hospital. Is it all right?" It was, and after imparting swift kisses, Molly took Raj's arm. It was a sultry night. The falling light made the surrounding brick facades glow orange, but the heat of the day was reluctant to depart.

After five minutes she said, "Don't gossip about me. It's one thing I have to ask."

"We weren't gossiping," said Raj, not so much to defend himself, but because her slightest displeasure made him childishly afraid. "He was helping me figure you out."

"You're too used to figuring out patients," Molly said. "Don't make me your case. *Listen, act, feel.*" She said the words with a special emphasis that caught him off guard.

"I'm pretty obsessed with you. It's not a secret," he said. "You want me to pay more attention to you?"

"No. You pay attention like I'm fragile, like I'm a butterfly who's going to dissolve in your hands. You know why? Because it makes you feel safe." Raj knew she was right. In medical school insecure students learned that the quickest way not to be frightened by an avalanche of suffering is to throw yourself into it. Helpers make a secret bargain with God to remain unafraid if they help others enough.

They didn't speak for a while, and Raj grew easy. Once he felt settled, he told Molly about his interview for one of the four residency slots that was opening up in the hospital that fall.

"It's a bunch of senior therapists, very formal-acting," Raj explained. "They all smoke a pipe, say nothing, and keep you on pins and needles."

"They don't talk?" said Molly.

"Not if they can help it. You're meant to sweat, and no matter what you happen to say, they exchange little glances with each other. The kind guaranteed to make you feel like an idiot."

One of the interviewers had asked him, "Why do you think you would make a good psychiatrist?" It was Halverson, who also supervised the junior staff. Because of that Raj felt he had an edge. In Halverson's mind, Raj knew that this was the key question. A lot rode on his answer since it was assumed that every candidate was already bright and ambitious. All his memorized lines instantly flew out of Raj's head.

"Well," he faltered, "when people start screaming, I don't feel like running away. I'm willing to stay and listen."

For some mysterious reason this won the committee's murmured approval. Raj heard through channels that he was a front-runner for one of the four spots. "Did you snow them?" Habib had asked. He had gone through the same process the year before.

"No. I told them I wanted to hear what patients have to say," Raj had replied.

"Ah." Habib had acted as if this was truly canny. It was generally tossed around that Halverson and the other seniors were outdated. They believed a therapist should hear every patient out for as long as it took, no matter how meager the results. In modern psychiatry, on the other hand, a screaming patient is an advantage because his mouth is already open, all the easier to pop in a pill. Then his therapist can feel good about walking away.

"That's very weird," Molly commented when Raj finished telling her. "You got through the question, but did you really have a reason?"

"Yeah. I'm not great at it yet, but therapy is a way to give people better ways to be human," said Raj. "I really believe that."

"You have a good heart," said Molly.

"You make it sound like a good heart falls short of something else," said Raj.

"A good heart doesn't fall short of anything," said Molly. "In your case, it's what makes you tick."

"What makes you tick?" said Raj. "Something different?"

"I think so."

"Then tell me."

"I know you've been out of your mind wanting to know," said Molly. Her eyes roamed toward the endless parade of strangers on the sidewalk. "All those people," she said, "are carrying around lives they can understand. I never could. If I look like I understand, I'm pretending. And don't laugh, but pretending isn't something I like to do."

"Do you think anyone really understands?" said Raj.

"It wouldn't help if they do or don't," said Molly. "I'm waiting for something else."

"Tell me."

"I want to be the one who's called out," said Molly. "I'm not being mysterious. It's like demanding to be special, but not because you feel conceited or haughty or too good for normal life. I think everyone has this seed that stays buried until an invisible light hits it."

"And if the seed sprouts?" asked Raj.

"Then maybe I could understand why I'm here and what this is all about."

"Have you been called out yet?" Raj asked.

Molly laughed. "No. Sort of. Who knows?"

"Love calls people out," Raj reminded her, "so in a way I've received your wish." Molly turned her head back toward him. It wasn't the first time he had alluded to how much in love he was, but this time he seemed to be leveling a faint accusation.

Molly said, "Yes, love calls us out, but sometimes we go back anyway. Feelings fade. Then you might wind up further behind than before you fell in love."

"Ah, so you're trying to give me a warning," said Raj, but his voice was relaxed. In many ways their conversation fit together better than their bodies. It was the thing he could cherish until he found out how well their hearts would fit.

Surprisingly, when they got to the hospital Molly wanted to take the elevator up to the pavilion. She didn't like hospitals on principle, and while they were making their way through the ER, she had clung close to Raj, avoiding eye contact with the critically bored and wounded waiting to be seen.

Raj punched the elevator button and watched the light coming down from the sixth floor. "If you hate it down here, why would you want to go up there?" he said.

"Because they're going somewhere I don't know about," said Molly. "These people are just sick."

"Not everyone up there is out of their minds. Most of them aren't, actually."

"Just let me see. I can be a visitor, can't I?"

"Sure, for a moment." They got onto the elevator and said nothing on the slow, swishing ride up. When the doors opened Molly commented on how dim the light was.

"It's supposed to be soothing," said Raj. "And their bedtime is at eight."

At the station Mona looked up and smiled, but Joanie didn't. *(Still chewing on the past,* Raj thought. *Or another date that didn't put out.)* "This is Molly," said Raj nervously.

Giving away nothing, Mona nodded. "Welcome to the last place on earth," she said. Joanie kept her head in her charts. She seemed to be holding back any vibe, good or bad.

"So this is where they keep them," Molly murmured, looking around.

"Not enough of them," said Mona. "It's a crime how

many walking wounded are on the streets. Up here are mostly people with families who can afford it."

Molly nodded and stepped away from the desk, heading down the corridor. Mona silently mouthed the word "pretty!" and Raj felt more nervous. As he followed Molly down the hall, the melancholy of the twilight hour hung over the ward. As she walked, Molly put her hand up to feel the walls, which were covered in red cloth to match the carpet. Raj wondered if she thought they should be padded. They reached the day room, which was around the corner at the end of the hall. Raj was about to say something when he stopped and pulled Molly back. Before them was a tableau about to explode. Two women stood face to face. One had her hand raised and the other, caught off guard, was reacting too slowly to protect her face.

"Hey!" Raj yelled.

But neither looked his way. The younger woman, who was new on the floor and appeared to be about twenty, hurled a cup of black coffee at the older, who screamed and lurched backward.

"Nurse!" Raj called as he moved in. He knew instantly that the older one was Claudia, who slapped her assailant hard across the face. "You fucking whore! You've scalded me! Look at me!"

"I'm doing the work of God," wailed the younger

woman in a high singsong. Still gripping the Styrofoam cup, she shook it again in Claudia's face, unaware that she had already emptied it. Raj was able to pull her back before Claudia could strike her again.

"It's all right, Mrs. Klemper," Raj said firmly. "I'm here to take care of this."

"You have crazy people in here!" Claudia screeched. She brought her hands up to her face. "No one will be able to look at me again." And for the first time that Raj had ever seen, she burst out crying. Mona and Joanie arrived on the scene. The younger woman was thrashing in Raj's arms with fierce manic strength. She seemed all taut muscle and wire under his hands, like a wildcat. In a lower voice now she kept repeating, "I'm doing the work of God. I'm doing the work of God."

"Help me here, please," said Raj. Mona took one side and Joanie the other.

"This is Sasha," Mona said. "She's one of Dr. Mathers'." When the nurses tried to pull the young woman away, she began to moan and sagged to the floor, as inert as a sack of flour.

"What's she on?" Raj asked.

"I'll have to check her chart, but I don't think there are any special orders beyond her maintenance." said Mona. "Seconal and something for nausea. She threw up."

"What are you doing? I'm burning up here!" Claudia sobbed. Her face was inflamed with rage, but Raj had felt the last few drops of liquid in the cup; to his relief they were cold.

"You're just badly frightened," said Raj, not wanting two patients out of control. "Feel your skin. The coffee wasn't scalding."

"The hell it wasn't!" Claudia rode a new surge of ire and tried to kick Sasha as the nurses pulled her to her feet.

"You're going to have to calm down," Raj said, hauling Claudia back. "I can walk you to your room. If you stay here it will just remind you." The crisis was cooled down enough that he could spare a look over his shoulder. Molly was standing about ten feet away; she was very still, her eyes fixed on Sasha. As the nurses walked her past, Raj thought he saw Molly reach out, only to stop at the last moment.

"Wait here," he said. "I'll be right back. Unless you want to go." Molly shook her head, and Raj coaxed Claudia away from the day room. Once she had calmed down a bit, he checked in at the nurses' station.

"What was she doing, this Sasha?" he asked Mona.

"Anointing people, I guess." Mona shrugged. "There's a lot of private communication with God going on today."

"Does Dr. Mathers know that his patient is prone to this kind of agitation?" asked Raj.

"He's talking to her about it," Joanie said, coming up behind them. "He cut back the dosage to see if he might have better ideas about what was wrong. But you might want to go in there. She's pretty bad." Joanie kept a straight face; Raj couldn't tell if she was hiding her opinion about Mathers or about him.

"One of you go to the cabinet and follow me with some Haldol," Raj ordered. "I'll see if I can get her to drink it, but otherwise we may have to inject. And see how much she's already taken of the Seconal. She's not going to stop freaking out until we settle her down."

On his way to Sasha's room, Raj read in her chart that she had suffered her first schizophrenic break at eighteen, five years before. The attending who admitted her had scribbled down a list of antipsychotic drugs she was supposed to be on; Sasha had a hard time tolerating them, but when she went off, her episodes recurred, with increasing signs of paranoia each time.

When Raj entered, the room was black. He heard a soft whimpering from one corner, and by the dim glow of the hallway lamps, he made out a crouching form.

"Sasha? I'm Dr. Rabban, and I'm here to help you," Raj said softly. "To do that I need to see you. I won't turn on all the lights, just one." Carefully he walked over and flicked on the fluorescent bar behind the bed. It buzzed to life, casting a greenish glare on the terrified young woman huddling on the floor. When he knelt down to raise her to her feet, Raj noticed how cold the air was down there.

"I am doing the work of God," Sasha said in barely a whisper.

"All right, but we want to get you better. You need to be back on your old meds," Raj said gently. The fire and sinew had drained out of her body; she felt limp as he lowered her into bed. Then her limbs went stiff, and her expression contorted itself into a silent shriek. It was the two-faced demon of paranoia, which brings the shining illumination of God one minute and unbearable torment the next.

Mona appeared by Raj's side, holding out a small metal tray with two bottles on it.

"Set them down," said Raj. "I want to observe her a few more minutes before I decide." He was flying in the dark with a hyper-agitated patient he had barely met. Five minutes didn't help; she continued to writhe and mumble. He thought about paging Mathers, but what good would it do? He had known Sasha for a couple of hourly sessions at best.

Raj opened the bottles and tapped a capsule of barbiturates and Thorazine into his palm. He poured a glass of water from the plastic pitcher by the bedside and lifted Sasha's head. "Here we go," he said softly, as if to a small child.

She opened her eyes, which had dark rings around them, and repeated her song of agony. "God is working through me. Who is working through you?"

"I'm not as lucky as you," Raj murmured. "There's no one working through me but me."

He would have opened her pursed mouth with his fingers and laid the pills on her tongue, but someone came into the room. He turned around and saw that it was Molly.

Raj said, "How long has it been? I didn't mean to leave you alone up here." He nodded toward Sasha, who saw Molly and instantly became more agitated. "She's going to be okay. You'd better leave."

Molly ignored him and came closer. She placed a hand on Sasha's body. "I don't think you should do this," she said. Raj didn't like any mental patient to be touched, but before he could say so, Molly added, "She's pregnant."

"How do you know? She's not showing."

"No one will know until you do a test, but sometimes I have a feeling," said Molly. "Would those pills hurt a pregnant woman?"

"Yes, they could be quite dangerous, in fact," said

Raj. He drew his hand back from Sasha's mouth and grabbed her chart. He hadn't missed anything; there was no note about her being pregnant.

"She's not married," he mumbled. But he knew that made little difference. Schizophrenics were easily abused sexually when others found out how little they could defend themselves. Molly stayed by the bed, but as if sensing his anxiety, she didn't touch Sasha again.

"If you just want her to sleep, I think she's going to," Molly said. She reached up and flicked off the fluorescent bar. "If anyone can with that hideous light on." Molly gave no outward sign that she was saying or doing anything extraordinary, but Raj could check out her guess with a pregnancy test. He thought for a second. In the dark he heard Sasha breathing slowly in soft, regular waves. It would do no harm to let her sleep. He would be on call in case she began to do God's work at three A.M.

"Okay," he whispered and led Molly back into the hall. They were silent on the way back to the nurses' station. Raj deposited Sasha's chart and said, "Let me walk you to the elevators. We're getting together tomorrow, right?" Molly nodded, and without asking her, he could tell the incident had caused wheels to turn. When they were away from the nurses, he said, "I've asked you to love me in more ways than I know how."

"I know," Molly said.

"In the restaurant, Bradley told me you were special. It took someone very sensitive to know if that girl might be pregnant. Are you waiting for a man who's more like you?"

"No, it's not that," she said. "Whatever I'm waiting for, I can't help it."

Raj groaned inside. He heard Joanie's voice calling from behind them. "Did you mean to leave this blank?"

"What?" Raj turned around, irritated.

Joanie was waving the chart. "You didn't mark down what you gave her."

"That's because I didn't give her anything," said Raj. "Just hold on, I'll be there."

"The bottles were open," said Joanie. "Should I wake up Dr. Mathers?"

"I said I'll be there," barked Raj. Joanie all but smirked. He knew that she was pulling something—another passive aggressive trick to make him look bad in front of Molly? He could hear the elevator whooshing up toward them.

"Every person is as deep as a well," said Molly. "But men keep the well capped. When I met you, you crashed through, and I thought that maybe the cap was coming off. I'm not going to dive into the dark, so I'm waiting."

"And while you wait, what am I supposed to do?" asked Raj.

"Don't worry," Molly said, brushing his cheek with her hand. "If a crazy girl thinks God is working through her, how far behind can you be?"

"Don't take that too seriously," said Raj. "It's schizoform thinking. She'll feel cursed in the morning."

Molly stepped into the car. "And I didn't mean to upset you by saying I was still looking for something. Because I think I may be seeing it."

"I love you," whispered Raj.

The doors closed, and Raj felt a release in his chest, just the feeling a patient must experience when his doctors find that the fatal X ray was a mistake. Raj would remember Molly's words for a long time. He headed back to the nurses' station to see how close he'd let himself get to wringing Joanie's neck.

5.

WHEN THE MORNING staff meeting came around, there was some hell to pay. Everyone sat in the office off of the nurses' station with black coffee, making small talk and watching Clarence review the charts of each patient on the floor. He had gotten to the last one without comment, flicking doughnut crumbs out of his beard. Generally, not much happened overnight.

"You might want to go back to that one," Mona remarked.

"Sasha Blum," said Clarence, scanning down the page. "Pregnancy test?" He turned to Raj. "This girl chose to reveal to you in the middle of the night that she was with child?"

"No one said anything about it to me," Mathers piped up. He was a first-year resident with straight blond hair and Yale ties. Raj barely knew him. "She's one of mine, a screaming zonker," said Mathers. Clarence kept looking at Raj, waiting for an answer.

"This girl was temporarily taken off her medications to see how she might respond, on Dr. Mathers' orders," Raj said, "and I found indications that she might be pregnant."

"From her? From the family? Who?" said Clarence.

"After I got on the floor, the nurses told me that she had thrown up earlier, and it seemed like a good idea to check," said Raj.

Clarence held up the chart, still scowling. "That's reasonable enough, but aren't we leaving out a full-blown psychotic episode? The order on the chart is to resume meds at the first sign of a relapse. You chose to ignore that. Why?" Raj looked startled and glanced over at Mathers.

"Because resuming meds wasn't on the chart last night," Raj said.

"Yes, it was. I wrote it before I went home," said

Mathers. "I wouldn't leave her hanging out to dry like that. You must have been in a hurry."

Raj felt himself tighten with anger. Before he could react, Mathers turned to Clarence. "Things got pretty hairy, I hear, and Raj had just come on service. No criticism—we all know it happens."

Bodies shifted uncomfortably around the table, and Raj reddened. Mathers had absolutely left Sasha hanging, and Raj thought he knew who had tipped him off to his blunder. Clarence pulled a yellow slip from the back of the chart. "You're a good guesser, Rabban. The test was positive. You and Mathers can now consult on what to do with a pregnant woman in the midst of a schizophrenic break."

"I already know what I want to do," Raj said quickly.

"And what is that?" Clarence asked.

"Whoa," Mathers interrupted. "Isn't she still my patient?"

"Suddenly you can't wait to care for a screaming zonker, as you so elegantly put it?" said Clarence. Mathers drew back with a wave of his hand.

"I'd like to sit with Ms. Blum for the rest of the day," said Raj carefully. "I'm still on, and there's not much other action on the ward. If you'll let me give her some personal attention, maybe I can determine who the father is and also judge how severe her current episode might be."

Clarence nodded and pushed the chart across the table. "All yours, but make a report to Mathers before you leave. Then he'll check in with me. Any more business, people? All right, let's go out there and cure one for the Gipper. Class dismissed."

Raj was still seething as he left the meeting. For Mathers to lie about the altered chart was a breach of ethics, but Sasha Blum had shoved Raj into a gray area as well. He couldn't very well tell Clarence that his new girlfriend sensed his patient's pregnancy. He had better just drop it. Going into her room, he found Sasha lying in bed outside the sheets, her back to the door. The pulled drapes let in a crack of sunlight that cut across her body like a harsh blade.

"Sasha?" he said tentatively.

"She's not here."

"I think she might be," said Raj, thankful that the woman responded to her name. "Can I talk to you? I have some news." There was no movement as Raj sat down on the edge of the bed. But time was too short to coax out and evaluate every marginal response. "I have what I hope is good news. You're going to have a baby."

"I'm going to die," Sasha said after a pause.

"Can you look at me?" Raj asked gently. Slowly Sasha rolled over, folding a gaunt arm across her face despite the darkened room. *She's in no mood to see what she has to see,* thought Raj. "Do you understand what I just told you?" he asked.

"My teacher carried me into the mountains," said Sasha, her face still covered. "Some of us ate out of the fields, others drank out of the forest. Nights have more feet. Can Miss Havisham hear the bombers?"

Raj waited. The words and images seemed loosely coherent, but he knew enough not to jump in and try to converse about whatever fantasy Sasha was dangling. Looking below the surface, the images were about danger and getting to safety. *She must feel very much in danger with this baby.*

"Do you understand what I just told you?" Raj repeated.

"The mountains are too cold to raise a child in," mumbled Sasha. "Blue jackets are warmer. Green is big." The arm came down. Her face was a mask showing no feeling, but at least it was not the contorted mask she had been wearing.

"I think you do understand, and you want to run away from it," Raj guessed out loud. "You know just where you want to run to. I won't stop you, but can we talk a little first? It's important."

The arm wavered like a curtain deciding whether to close. One of the first clichés a shrink learns concerns the difference between a neurotic and a psychotic. A neurotic is someone who builds castles in the air; a psychotic is someone who moves into them. The punch line is, "And a psychiatrist is someone who gathers the rent." Raj knew that Sasha was psychotic enough to retreat into a fantasy world—the events of the previous night left no doubt of that. So the only question was whether she had the willpower to come back down to Earth. If her disease forced her out of reality, he had no choice but to medicate her.

"Wave if you remember who I am," Raj said gently, hoping to make contact. A faint crack appeared in the mask, and her fingers gave a weak wiggle though her eyes were still afraid and exhausted beyond any measure a young girl deserved. Raj remembered what Halverson had said on the first day of training. "We're not here to save souls. That is impossible. It's not a temptation you are permitted. We're barely here to cure people, but that at least we can attempt." It was a lesson that was proving to be difficult for Raj to accept in this case.

"I go places," Sasha said.

"I know," said Raj.

"You don't. I go places when I stop taking my beds—
my meds," she stammered, making sense with obvious
difficulty. "Streets come in on cat's feet. Tippy and
trippy. One never knows. And sometimes I wake up
next to the last person on earth who would think I
pray, 'cause I do." *She wandered at night and woke up in the
morning next to strange men.*

"So the father is probably someone you don't know,"
said Raj gravely.

Sasha cringed. "We aren't accepting visits from Mrs.
Rude today. Tiddley-boo." Even as she withdrew, Raj
was lucky that she was reaching out to talk with him.
Her shipwrecked mind drifted before it found any
port of calm. He couldn't load her down right away
with all the tests they needed to run in a pregnancy
with so many possible risks, from AIDS to substance
abuse by the unknown father. "Do you have someone
we should call?"

Sasha hesitated. "In my pillow. My pillow's a bag. You
can look in my bag, but you can't take."

"Good, I'll have the nurses look in your bag. They
won't touch anything else." Sasha got up and walked
over as if to pull the drapes, but instead she leaned
against the wall. Raj knew she wouldn't cry, that such a
normal response would be impossible for her right now.

She had no access to the place where our true fears and desires lie deep with tears.

If she wandered the streets, he would have to sign orders for the drugs that would take the hallucinations away, but they would blank out more than her ravenous terror.

"We're going to do everything we can for you," said Raj. "I'll be back." As he turned to leave he heard Sasha flicker back into clarity. *"Every person is as deep as a well. I think that's what frightens me the most."* A shiver ran down Raj's spine at the echo of Molly's words. He could have stopped and asked what was happening, but how would Sasha know, she who was lucky to know what month it was? As he stepped into the corridor, Raj wondered if he was stupid. How many clues had he been given besides this one? What were they gesturing toward, as unmistakable as birdsong or animal cries and equally unintelligible?

"Has the UFO landed?"

Raj looked up to see Mathers. "More or less," said Raj. "She's not altered, but we can't take her off the drugs. Sasha got pregnant because she stopped medicating herself and began to go into fugue states."

Mathers shrugged. "We tried."

Seeing the look on Raj's face, he added, "I know you think I'm being insensitive. I took her off meds hoping she'd surface. Sometimes they quit flying the friendly skies given half a shot. How many walking psychotics do we see a day—a dozen? twenty? Some of them handle their lives pretty well. But this thing is what it is. After she takes her pills tonight, she won't even remember that there was a today."

Raj wondered how many times Mathers could keep saying "she" without using Sasha's name. "What about her baby?" he said.

"We'll just have to see," said Mathers. "If I was her, I'd lose it. A lot of schizophrenics forget there's even a baby in the house or that it belongs to them. If she's indigent, social services and the courts could force her to lose it. As I recall, she comes from family and goes to a good college here in the city. She's lucky, she'll have more options."

Raj could see that Mathers wasn't trying to go toe-to-toe. He wasn't as callous as he put on, and whatever motives had influenced him to go into psychiatry, they approximated Raj's own reasons. He was also intuitive enough to take a crack at reading Raj's mind.

"That's right," Mathers said. "I'm one of the good guys. Try to get used to that fact. It's a symptom of a borderline personality to see things in black-and-white. So you want to smoke a peace pipe or get some coffee?"

"We still need to have that consult about managing Sasha from now on."

"I thought we just did. She's back on Clozapine, we put her under close watch until it kicks in, just in case she decides to spray holy water again, and then whoever usually takes care of her signs her out to take care of her some more." Mathers looked impatient and busy, and technically Raj couldn't blame him.

"All right," Raj conceded. Looking satisfied, Mathers walked away, but Raj pulled him back. "One more thing. If you're going to hook up with Joanie," he said, "next time don't have her fix your charts, okay? Now maybe I can have a free hand with this girl Sasha? I think I deserve that much."

Mathers narrowed his eyes, and Raj wondered if he would deny the accusation. But all he said, with a small mirthless smile, was, "Do what you think you can. Sasha's lucky to have you."

RAJ BROKE HIS promise to himself. He didn't confess to Maya. Besides her grandfather's illness, she faced a great deal of stress at work. Her career choice suited her very well, but Maya was too softhearted.

"You're going to be spending a lot of time in court and a lot more in purgatory with these people," said Raj over dinner. She had brought take-out curry up to his apartment.

"Am I supposed to cut myself off from what I feel?" asked Maya.

"Sometimes, yes. The courts have to find you credible, whether you advise that a family can be put back together or whether they have to be split up," Raj said.

"It's sickening. Maybe I'm not cut out for this," said Maya sadly. "And then there's us."

Raj felt his throat tighten. "What do you mean?" he said.

"I'm not sure a marriage can stand two people working with so much misery, day in and day out. It's too much to ask. I notice it already."

"Since when?"

Raj realized that he was setting himself up, but he couldn't help it. His guilt egged him on.

"I can't be specific. But whatever they're doing to you, you're not the same," said Maya. "Forget it. I'm just adding to your troubles."

Raj took her hand, not because he wanted to, but because he knew he would have before he met Molly. "I'm not troubled, Maya. I'm—"

He didn't pause for lack of courage. Once she knew everything, Maya might accuse him of cowardice. But it wasn't that, not as Raj saw it. Love had betrayed him. It was pulling him in different directions, toward two very different women, and although decency made him want to choose, love refused to let him. Its gentle side turned Maya into the woman he most wanted. Its enigmatic side turned Molly into the same thing. It would be cruel and ridiculous to tell Maya that she wasn't mysterious enough. That wasn't the problem. Goodness can't be thrown away because it doesn't have secrets. Only now that the crisis was at hand, mystery was Raj's last excuse.

"There's someone else," he said.

Maya put down her fork and hung her head. "How long?" she asked softly.

"A while. You know her—well, you know who she is."

Maya looked shocked. "Who do you mean?" she asked.

"The actress we saw that night. Her name's Molly," said Raj.

"It wasn't that hard to sense. I was just hoping I was wrong." Maya got up and quickly found her things, pushing Raj away when he tried to touch her.

"I always felt your hesitation," she said, and the words came out practiced, as if she had already envisioned this moment. "So it's not her fault. You wanted someone else from the beginning."

"That's not true," said Raj.

"Oh, shut up!" Maya flared. "If you're going to have your way, at least let me talk. You were cruel to take me to see her that night. That was unforgivable. It was torture once you left at intermission. I wanted to believe you had an emergency, but my heart said something else. I couldn't say anything to you. You were the one I loved. I just kept telling myself that my heart was mistaken. I was even glad in a small way that my parents left suddenly and I was lonely, because it gave you a chance to show that you still cared."

"And I did. I still do care," said Raj miserably.

"No, that's just what you like to call feelings," said Maya. "Two steps forward, one step back. It's the same story and I'm getting to know it well. I realize a person can't have everything. To me you were wonderful, and just this moment I have seen how cruel you can be. See, feelings change!" Maya broke down into tears. Letting them run down her face, she threw on her knapsack and headed for the door. Weeping blinded her; she fumbled with the double latch.

"Here," Raj said.

"Don't!" Maya cried. But in the end, even as her crying became uncontrollable, she had to let him throw the lock. Raj saw her running down the hall with both hands over her mouth, so the neighbors wouldn't hear.

Hating himself, he phoned Molly and begged her to come over. He was both obsessed and thwarted by love. Molly was surprised to hear from him. "You sound strange," she said on the phone.

"Don't ask me any questions," he said. "Not tonight. Just come over."

Molly agreed without hesitation, but the moment she walked in, she again asked, "What's the matter?"

"It's not something we have to talk about. Just be with me."

They made love in a different way that night. Raj felt her presence, something beyond her body; Molly clung to him as if she meant to convey that she was not one of the many dim forms pressing into his reality while never quite entering it. She had never said, "Touch me here," or "Slower now," and she didn't tonight. Her flesh itself seemed to tell him what she wanted, and his flesh understood. Because they were both tired, the physical act itself changed, and to Raj's surprise, the fatigue in his limbs made things better. It was his languorous weight sliding across her, not the weight of the world, and his mind, too dulled to keep vigil over his performance, finally relaxed.

He didn't dare speak in the first moments afterward. But instead of drifting with him into a sated dream, Molly sat up. She looked very alert.

"That was—" She paused, and for a second Raj braced himself. "That was the first time you weren't making love to *her,*" said Molly. Raj started, thinking she meant Maya. But he remembered: Molly referred to her acting persona as *her.* Before Raj could respond, Molly put her fingers over his lips. It was all she wanted to say, all she wanted said. And within a few seconds, Raj's flesh understood this, too.

It was the kind of sex that led to exhilaration, at least for her. Once he was no longer holding her, Raj felt the tip of a knife in his chest. But he allowed himself to be pulled out into the streets. The night sky was amazingly clear, spread overhead like a velvet banquet. They had no idea where they were going, but like pilgrims drawn to the river, they headed for Broadway. The crowds of a summer night were bustling.

"Let's just follow these distracted wanderers," said Molly, waving at the packed throng. She was too high to feel jostled or pressed. The swarm of humanity flowed downtown. Love performs so many miracles that the minor ones are often casually overlooked. Raj was recovering. He was totally bewildered, yet he noticed that the traffic looked beautiful, like glowing chariots in a world of grimy dented wagons. All because of her.

In the upper Seventies they passed a late-night delicatessen, and suddenly Molly was famished. They went inside and roamed around. Molly was enjoying herself at the glass fish counter, where it looked as though every creature of the sea had been perfectly sliced and smoked. Off to one side an argument broke out. A middle-aged man in a white apron, red-faced and harsh, was yelling at a cowering girl who looked about eighteen.

"What are you, some kind of lamebrain?" the man shouted. "You don't know the difference between six ninety-nine and sixty ninety-nine? You know how much money I could lose?" The girl hung her head, and her lip quivered.

"It was a mistake. I'll take care of it," she mumbled.

"Goddam right you'll take care of it! You think anybody else would hire someone like you? Do you? Gimme a break." The man's rage seemed out of proportion. People in the near vicinity moved out of range, except for Molly, who slid along the fish counter to get closer. She kept looking at the stacks of pink salmon with their wide, black eyes and the squid that look like flattened gray balloons.

"Dad," the girl pleaded. She looked humiliated but unable to turn away. The tension in the air made her back into a pyramid of quail eggs in jars, and several crashed to the floor. This seemed to fuel the man's anger even further.

"Christ! You're going to clean that up and pay for every one of them, you hear me? As far as I'm concerned, your whole life is a waste!" The girl had started to cry now. She knelt on the floor trying to gather up the smashed glass and pickled eggs sloshing in their brine. The crazed martinet who was apparently her father stood over her, glaring and keeping watch in case he needed to fire another round at her.

Molly had watched the entire scene intently. Now she walked up to the man and his daughter, who were separated by barely a foot, and threaded her way between them. They looked startled, and for a second Raj thought the man would lash out at Molly. Then she paused for a second, studying the labels on some cans as if they were the most absorbing reading in the world. Raj could feel the tension ease, and the girl stopped crying. Even the man's body lost its rigidity. In a few seconds, Molly was back by his side.

"What did you do?" he asked. Molly gave him a *"You'll see"* smile and said, "I'm ready to leave."

On the way out, she gestured to the left with her head. Raj glanced over. The man in the apron was crouching to help clean up the mess. He was smiling and joking with a few customers, and his daughter laughed with him. There was nothing amazing in the sight, unless you had witnessed the scene before.

"I changed them," Molly said.

"How? You just walked between them."

"I took on what they were feeling, and then I let it go," she said.

"Why?"

"Because they couldn't. Not by themselves. It's like trapped steam. Their emotions were so strong neither one could let go without being afraid that they would bust a gasket." Molly tugged at Raj's arm and pulled him out of the shop.

"How can you be sure?" he demanded. "Maybe they just calmed down."

"I used to do the same thing with my parents when they had a fight. I can't remember how it started; it just did," said Molly, holding out a biscotti. When Raj pushed it away, she nibbled on it herself. "I admit it's strange, but unlike you I don't indulge in the fantasy that life is normal, ever."

"What makes you think that I do?"

"Well, for one thing, it rattles your cage that I might be right about this. You can't just observe and accept it. You feel that life has to be normal, so you push this away."

Raj couldn't deny what she was saying, although there was another ingredient: his fear that every time she showed him something scary, she was trying to move away from him. He caught himself. *Why do I think it's scary?*

Molly answered the question for him. "Normal life doesn't really exist, only predictable life. What you can't predict, you also can't control. And that frightens people out of their gourds."

"So why are you immune?" he asked.

"I'm not. I was scared of you when you broke into my dressing room. But when I feel that something can't be controlled, I look closer instead of running away."

"That's good," Raj said.

Molly laughed. "You can't imagine how consoling it is to have your approval." She seemed nonchalant, forgetting the incident as quickly as it arose. But for the next ten blocks Raj kept feeling a strange ferment inside. He recalled his own parents fighting. When he was six or seven, their small domestic battles caused terror in him. He would run to his room and bury his head in a pillow, his eyes squeezed as tight as possible. He imagined that most children used this kind of fearful denial. It was a defense against helplessness. Molly didn't give in to helplessness; she had found a different way. Raj thought of Sasha Blum, so bereft that any trace of a living girl had been stripped from her as if with an iron rake. And he saw that like her, he was in danger of viewing the world as a place where everything can be lost instead of a place where everything might be found.

"I saw a strange patient yesterday," Raj said suddenly. "He was an older guy, living in a shelter most of the time, who had been pulled out of an abandoned building. At first they thought he was scrounging for crack, but he wasn't. He kept telling everyone that the abandoned building was Roseland, and then someone realized he meant the old dance hall that used to be near Times Square.

"So of course they assumed he was nuts and I got called down. 'Mr. Schirmer,' I asked, 'why did you go back to Roseland?' And he told me that was where he took his wife to dance many years ago. 'So you went there to remember better times,' I said. He gave me this blank look and he said, 'I go back to dance with her again.'

"It turns out she died in the shelter last month. So I had a syringe in my hand, ready to shoot some tranquilizers into his IV, and I saw as clear as day what I was doing. I was about to deprive this guy of the reason he was living. I was taking away Roseland with a simple plunge and a squirt."

"And did you?" asked Molly. She looked away, not wanting the answer. "I wouldn't have."

Raj pulled her around. "It wasn't such a simple

choice, Molly. You don't have my job." He had a catch in his throat. "I was giving him peace and calm."

"At a price," she said.

"Sure, okay. Have it your way. I imagine he'll see his wife again tomorrow or next week. Whenever the dose wears off."

"I'm glad for her," said Molly cryptically.

The shadows had only passed over her for a moment. Molly and Raj wended their way back uptown. The blocks became grayer and more bare, like the side of a mountain when the lush valleys are left behind. It was the first time they fell asleep on the verge of making love. Exhausted as they were, neither wanted to be the one who said no, so they woke up with their limbs wrapped around each other the next morning as tangled as passion vines.

OVER THE NEXT few days, a new idea came to Raj. It applied first to Sasha Blum and then began to spread. He wondered if everyone—even the crazies—was just the fragment of a soul reaching out for love.

"Why have we given up on touching people?" he asked Habib. "What makes their desperation so different from ours or anyone's?"

"If you mean patients," said Habib, "a lot of them aren't in radio contact. They can't be touched."

"When was the last time you told a patient that you felt the same way he did?"

"Well, this morning I saw Mr. McPatrick, who is sixty. His daughters brought him in because he went on a trip without his lithium, and once he hit his manic phase, he felt so terrific that he proposed to two airline attendants on the same flight. I'd have a hard time looking deep into his eyes and telling him I feel like that sometimes."

"So you would never try to get close to a patient, no matter how much they needed human contact?" said Raj.

"If you love them up," warned Habib, "you'll get eaten alive."

Almost everyone on the pavilion floor agreed with Habib. The rise of drug therapy had made it easier to treat patients without being touched by them, or touching them in return. One holdout, however, was Halverson. He had been forced to bow to the usefulness of drugs, but he would not surrender his deep faith that the mind was sacred.

"I can take two depressed patients," Halverson told the young doctors who were under him, "and relieve the symptoms of the first one with Prozac or any number of related pills. The results will be quick and often very complete. The second patient I can talk to. I can get him to see what has made him depressed, and the results will be slow and often very incomplete. But here's the difference. If you take that first patient off Prozac, his symptoms will return immediately in full force, whereas the second patient has at least a chance of making progress toward a cure. Aren't we here to cure people?"

The debate was thirty years old but still passionate. Whenever Raj, who saw himself close to Halverson on the matter, argued with Habib, his friend scoffed in his face. "Your shaman is wrong. We are here to relieve suffering, and all this stuff about unraveling the psyche is just an excuse. Why should a patient remain in pain waiting for his shrink to map the dungeons of his mind? It's ridiculous."

"My shaman may believe that there's a ghost in the machine," countered Raj, "but it's a hell of a lot better than a machine with nothing inside."

None of this crystallized until Molly came into his life. As Raj went through his own sea change, he saw the pavilion as a zone of no love, a gray world of aching misery and detached helpers. Why did he have to obey the rule that said never to tell patients anything personal? Therapists drone on every day that emotions are good, positive things, only to turn around and make sure their own are kept completely out of reach. A new feeling was rising in Raj, almost a demand. If he was in love, and that love made him ride waves of hope and joy, why couldn't he tell people who had lost even a vision of hope and joy?

Habib heard him out and said, "You're asking for trouble, amigo."

The next time Raj walked into Sasha Blum's room, she was sitting in a chair smoking a cigarette, dressed in black jeans and a frilly top. Her face was made up, and the instant Raj entered, her head tilted back and she laughed at something someone just said.

"Hello again," she practically chirped. "I have visitors. See?"

"You're up," said Raj, "that's good."

"More than up," Sasha replied without hesitation.

Raj thought she looked like a rag doll that someone had painted and thrown on the chair. He barely had a moment to adjust to her strange transformation. Sasha's two visitors regarded him. One was a young man with a goatee who immediately pushed his hand forward. Raj didn't reach out to shake it, because his eyes were fixed on the other visitor.

"This is strange," the other one said. It was Maya. She

was sitting on the edge of Sasha's bed, casually dressed with blue sunglasses pushed up into her black hair, which was pulled back and tied. She didn't get up when she saw Raj. Instead, holding up a pack of cigarettes, she said, "I guess these aren't allowed? Sasha asked for them."

"It's okay," said Raj, coming to and taking the young man's hand to shake. It was a feeble, cold handshake, and his immediate impression was that the person attached to it must be timid and unsure of himself.

"I'm Barry, Sasha's friend," the young man said. "From school."

Raj ignored him. "How have you been?" he asked Maya.

Maya stuffed the cigarettes back into her black knapsack and with a sideward glance said, "I'm Sasha's friend, but I'm her caseworker, too. She's doing well."

"I really am," exclaimed Sasha. For the moment she was the most self-possessed one in the room. "Dr. Rabban is the person who can tell me when I go home. Something to do with blood tests."

Raj brought his attention back to her. "Just the first one," he said. "We screen your blood here first. You can come in every couple of weeks for the others. It's to keep your medication in balance." He kept his eyes off Maya, hoping she could find her composure. She hadn't

returned his calls since his confession. Nothing was settled, yet Raj felt a strange joy at seeing Maya again, as if
a net were drawing him back to her, but the net
wouldn't catch him; he knew that, too.

"I'll be bringing Sasha in for those tests," said Maya.
"You can give me the details. Do I have to sign
something?"

"Maybe, I'll check on it," Raj mumbled. Barry, whoever he was, seemed to sense sparks in the room, which
he reacted to by picking up a portable phone from the
bedside table and fiddling with it. Sasha coasted on her
good mood. "Dr. Rabban has been by my side every
minute," she said. "He understands me."

"I'm sure," said Maya. "He looks like he has a lot of
empathy." She took out a Kleenex and gently wiped a
small smear of brilliant red lipstick from the corner of
Sasha's mouth.

"Actually, Sasha," Raj broke in. "You may have
caught that Maya and I know each other. Very well, in
fact. But I'm glad you have someone you can rely on.
She's very trustworthy."

"Although somewhat too trusting," said Maya. She
reached for Sasha's cigarette. "Two more puffs, and then
we're leaving," she said tersely.

"Can I see you in the hall for a second?" Raj asked.
Maya looked startled but nodded. When they got out-

side Raj said, "We need to be extra cautious around Sasha. I don't know how well you know her, but she was brought in a few days ago in a seriously altered state."

"Are you implying that my behavior is out of line?" Maya said. She didn't flare up but kept her voice steady and her eye fixed on Raj's face.

"I wasn't implying anything," he said. "She's fragile, and I don't want her to be exposed to undue tension." Raj had no trouble reading Maya's doubts: *Since when did you develop this tenderness about anyone's feelings?*

"How did you wind up with Sasha?" he said.

Maya was uncomfortable, but she told Raj that she had met Sasha at school. Sasha went to NYU and lived in the dorms. Such kids, when they felt troubled, could go to a campus counseling service, where Maya had lately started working.

"So you're responsible for looking after Sasha's welfare?" asked Raj.

"Not to that extent. I like Sasha, and we're friends."

Raj took all this in. "And Barry?"

"He's more than casual but less than serious. They're lab partners or something. It's that age," said Maya. "I haven't told him anything about Sasha's problems, if that's what you're getting at."

"Why does he think Sasha is here?"

"She's depressed about finals and afraid she might have a drinking problem."

A burst of loud laughter poured from the room, and they both paused. Raj wondered if this merriment struck Maya as bizarre. He didn't really know how involved she was with Sasha. He took the risk of a small foray.

He said, "I'd like to deal with you personally in this case." Seeing Maya stiffen, he quickly added, "We'd have to set aside our recent . . . incident. That doesn't mean glossing over the problem. It's entirely your call."

"Incident? You make it sound like an incursion into Iraqi air space," she shot back, showing just the edge of the bitterness she'd been hiding.

"Iraq is probably less hostile right now," said Raj, trying to make a wry joke. Maya's face went stony. "I never stop regretting any harm I did to you," he said. "Believe me." Raj knew it wasn't the time or place for his words to sound believable.

"And?" said Maya.

"I was just hoping I could be frank with you. Patients like Sasha are basically maintained on drugs, but she has a tendency to go off them, and then—"

"I know a bit about that," Maya interrupted. "Not

much. But if what you're dancing around is whether I know she's schizophrenic, the answer is yes. I think I'm about the only one she's told at school."

Maybe, Raj thought, *but you don't know she's pregnant, and I can't tell you, not yet.*

"What do you think of her behavior today?" asked Raj.

"She's pretending. She wants to get out of here, and she looks upon me and Barry as her allies. People who might help convince the powers that be that she's okay. Do you see anything wrong with that? It's a mark of sanity not to want to stay in this place." Maya said these words soberly, but with the slightest hint of defiance against Raj.

"It isn't necessarily sane to want to leave here," he said. "But you're right."

"What are you two doing out here—conspiring?"

Sasha had come to the door. Her voice sounded bright, but Raj could see anxiety in her eyes. She was definitely as fragile as he had warned Maya, he thought with a stab of pity. It was not a professional emotion, yet he had to follow it. He was going to draw Sasha into his net, as tenderly as possible, and then give her back a self, exactly what Halverson said a therapist shouldn't be tempted to do.

"You busted us, we were conspiring," said Maya. "To

see how early you can leave. I told Dr. Rabban here that
you check in with me quite often and that you know
pretty much what your situation is."

Sasha nodded, the tenseness visibly subsiding in her
body. As close as they had been, Raj was newly
impressed with Maya. Her ability to tell the truth under
pressure would be considered exceptional in any circle
of therapists. She would make a good ally—assuming
Raj could convince her not to be his enemy. The first
unexplained joy he felt upon seeing Maya washed over
him again.

"Here, I'll collect the evil weed," said Raj, holding
out his hand for the cigarette in Sasha's mouth, "and
who knows how quick you'll be able to get back home?
I feel you are in safe hands with Maya."

Sasha looked delighted. "I knew you'd understand—
you're lovely!" she squealed. She really was very warm
for a schizophrenic, Raj thought. Perhaps too warm, if
she ever figured out how to get around him.

The three agreed that Sasha could be picked up in
the morning and that Maya would accompany her
to the outpatient clinic. When they went back into the
room, Barry was still fiddling nervously with the phone,
apparently wishing that it was a video game.

As the visitors were leaving, Maya said to Raj, "I can
do something you don't know about." Raj was startled.

"I can forgive you—I think," said Maya. "I must have been part of the problem."

"You weren't," said Raj. "Trust me."

"Let's not get carried away," said Maya. She smiled sadly and left.

Raj followed her to the elevator with his eyes, wondering. They had been too composed. It was her composure that worried him most. Part of him had expected her to be devastated. She wasn't. Shouldn't he feel relieved? Why didn't he? It hit him that Maya might not actually have loved him that much. Or was her detachment a sign that she might have loved him more than he had ever realized?

For the first time, he felt really miserable. A sudden insight had flashed through his mind. He loved Molly and Maya equally. His parents had taught him that it was possible to deeply love many at the same time. Raj had passed this off as an exotic notion that didn't apply to him. Now he wondered if it might be true. *Is it possible to be deeply in love with more than one person at the same time?* If this deep love was radiating with such intensity from within him, going out to both Molly and Maya, why was he so miserable?

6.

EVEN THOUGH RAJ had convinced himself, somewhere deep inside his soul, that he loved two women, he
chose to immerse himself in Molly. He began to think
that there were only two kinds of people in the world:
lovers and everyone else. Love made him feel protected,
and he wanted Molly to be protected, too. He would
wake up in the middle of the night to watch her sleep,
brushing stray strands of hair away from her mouth, as if

this small gesture would make it possible for her to take her next breath.

Molly had told him that she was waiting for an invisible light to awaken her, to call her out from ordinary life. Raj felt that she was surrounded by such light. It made her sensitive and intuitive; it gave her a special beauty. When Molly's back was toward him in the bathtub, Raj pondered the rippled curve of her spine as if it were a miracle instead of the numbered vertebrae he had memorized in medical school.

Molly accepted all this gracefully. Sometimes it made her melancholy, however, as if Raj's eyes asked for too much. Out of the blue she once said, "An older man came backstage and gave me a tiny box of chocolate truffles. He said they cost six dollars each and were flown in every week from Zurich. He wouldn't go away until I tasted one. When I bit in, there were flecks of gold in it. The taste was exquisite. But if you put that truffle into a microwave for ten seconds, it would turn into a gooey puddle, just like that."

"Meaning what?" asked Raj.

"Don't rely on beauty. Remember that happiness depends on things that can be destroyed at a touch."

"But the essence would still be there," said Raj. "I believe that now. You'll never turn into a gooey puddle."

"You just enjoy being ridiculous," Molly replied wistfully.

Their lives were merging more every day; they lived like defectors or fugitives from everyone else's world. Living for each other gave their love a secrecy that Raj kept close all the time. Nothing bothered him now, except for his conscience whenever he thought about Maya. As much as he tried to drive her from his mind, it didn't work.

Raj felt his heart was softer; however, he saw that his patients were not benefiting. They remained enclosed in their stubborn fear and pain, with him the godlike doctor looking on. Few seemed to want Raj to come closer. Another cliché shrinks learn right away is that therapy is like prying open an oyster. The patient is going to use the last ounce of strength to stay clamped tight. That was the game.

The only patients who didn't refuse to see him were the occasional psychopaths like Bobby T. Bobby T. was a suburban teenager who had been brought in after stealing seven cars and spreeing across five states before hitting a pedestrian outside New Haven. The police brought him in for mental evaluation, a fairly normal routine with an eighteen-year-old whom no one was anxious to jettison into the criminal system.

"Do you know why you stole those cars? Were you feeling upset about something?" Raj began when Bobby T. was presented to him. The kid was in a good mood. He had been flirting with half the nurses, and Joanie had bought him a Coke. He was a tall, thin boy with a handsome face under a shock of disheveled black hair. "You got any rum to put in this?" he asked Joanie, and she just smirked. A natural charmer.

Bobby T. shrugged off Raj's question. "I needed a car. I was going to return it." He looked very unconcerned about being in trouble, even less so about lying. The truth was that when each of the seven cars ran out of gas, he ditched it and stole the next one.

Raj was thinking about how to write up some notes that would make this boy look like a confused teen who had temporarily lost control when Bobby T. said, "This is kind of a weird situation when you think about it."

"What do you mean?" asked Raj.

"I could go out of this room and say that you touched me—you know. I bet that would go a long way to getting me off." Bobby said this in a calm, even amused voice.

"You're right, that is weird," said Raj cautiously. His first thought was that Bobby T. was hinting at abuse in the past, a thing boys in particular find extremely painful to bring up. "But you know I am only here to help you, right?"

"I guess. You're pretty young, aren't you? And you look different from the other doctors. There's something going on with you." Bobby T. was grinning now. Raj worked hard not to wriggle in his chair. Psychopaths have incredible instincts for other people's weaknesses. They seize power very quickly and have no conscience about using it to their advantage, no matter who else they hurt.

"You're very resourceful," said Raj, trying for a small diversion. "I see you got several truckers to give you rides, and some even gave you money, right?"

Bobby T. wasn't misled. "If I were in your shoes, I would be feeling pretty uncomfortable right now. If I can get money out of dumb-ass truckers, who knows what I could get out of you." He paused to let his words sink in. "It would really be a help if you wrote down that I needed therapy or whatever. Because you know I do."

The ploy didn't work. Raj got out of the room after noting the boy's psychopathic tendencies in his chart, and Bobby T. was shuffled off somewhere in custody. But Raj felt fairly certain that if he hadn't cut off the interview, Bobby T. would have cried out that the doctor had touched him. The last words the boy said were, "You really look like you've got an itch you need to scratch, doc." The mysterious impression that he had been to the depths haunted Raj for the rest of the day. If a psychopath could see so much, then maybe a lot of the patients knew more than they were letting on. Could this be turned to good? Not unless Raj could make them stop pretending to be blind.

Raj surprised everyone at the weekly staff meeting by saying, "I need volunteers for an experiment."

"You're kidding," said Mathers, who knew that Raj disliked the drug-testing that went on in the hospital. "What are you going to do, put all the chronics on Midol and cookies?" Several people got a good chuckle at that.

"You're close," said Raj. He was gaining a reputation for successfully reducing the medication given to some of the more hopeless long-term patients on the ward. Several of the schizophrenics had not spoken in months or years. They sat for hours barely moving and had to be led to meals by hand. In therapy they gave no more response than a potted plant, and for all intents and purposes their families were warehousing them until the money ran out; then they would be shipped off to the state hospital. Everyone knew that these semi-human robots were kept that way by their medication. Their psychotic symptoms were so masked that it was possible that they weren't even crazy anymore, just drugged out. Not knowing the difference was the price one paid for keeping them quiet. A few had started coming back to life when Raj simply cut their dosage in half.

"I'm not thinking of drugs now," said Raj. "I'd like to take a few of the patients who aren't responding but who don't display flagrant symptoms all the time. They need motivation to get out of here. A lot of them never will because life on the ward is easy. It's retreat from reality with three squares a day and helpful people who give you sponge baths."

"We are treating these people, you know," Clarence pointed out. But he didn't stop Raj, who held up a piece of paper.

"I decided to make a list of all the feelings that our patients don't have. It's a long list, because most of them don't feel much beyond depression and anger. As we all know, patients push feelings away. They often use their bodies to turn feelings into aches and pains. They use words to fend us off when we ask emotional questions."

No one looked interested. Raj stopped and looked around. "I'm sensing resistance, so I'll cut this short. If any of you would like to join me in reaching out to a few patients, see me afterwards."

"Resistance isn't a good reason for stopping," said Clarence. "It's the reason we go on. I don't believe anyone here will scream if you try to pry us open a bit. What is your idea, exactly?" Raj had nothing to lose.

"Okay," he said. "We take the patient and meet with him in a sunny corner of the day room, someplace where the outside world can be seen, and we challenge him. 'Don't you want to be out there again?' One of us would be a doctor, but I also want a nurse present, and if the patient is a man, preferably a nurse he might be attracted to. Some of these patients have absolutely no enticement in their lives, yet all of us do. It's part of being normal. Let's get their blood going. And instead of listening to them whine and resist and play games, we won't end a session until they have shown at least one emotion that they were afraid to show before. Finally, and I know this will be a leap for a few of my colleagues, we will tell them that we have the same feelings as well."

There, he had said it. Sunny corners and lively nurses was one thing, but *the doctor is never to lose power to the patient.* Everyone knew that. It was the whole reason for not telling a patient about your personal life. No tears or smiles, no giving out of phone numbers and addresses, not a hint about who you loved or who had ever hurt you.

"They'll just get their rocks off thinking you're in love with them," said Mathers.

"That's if you're lucky," said another resident. "The manic ones will jump you in the hall."

"That bit about attractive nurses is sexist garbage," one of the nurses put in.

For all the wise words about keeping one's distance for the sake of the patient, Raj knew that they were basically afraid. Their power was their shield. It was the opposite side of the coin from the patients, whose weakness was their shield. Everyone around the table knew that, but instead of making the subject easier to discuss, they all jumped into their heads and had a thousand reasons why the system, even if imperfect, was right.

Raj was surprised the following week when he was approached by Joanie. "I want to be your first nurse," she said. "To do that thing."

"I thought my suggestion was canned," said Raj.

"No, I just asked one of the supervisors. It's okay to try it with a few patients, if you still want to, that is." She looked serious, and so far as Raj could tell, she wasn't coming on to him or acting quasi-seductive in any way.

"You're on," he said. Joanie smiled and rubbed up against him accidentally as she went down the hall. He had to remember to take people as they are.

A few hours later Claudia Klemper found herself next to the east window of the day room looking down on a magnificent sugar maple turning golden in the sun down below. "What the hell is this?" she asked.

"I thought it would be nicer to meet here for our session than in a dark office," said Raj. He and Joanie sat in easy chairs pulled in from the lounge. He offered a third to Claudia, who eyed it as if she had been told to sit on a barracuda. "Let's put it this way," said Raj. "It can't hurt to sit in a cheerful place, can it?"

"You mean because I have so damn much to be cheerful about?" grumbled Claudia, "what with my children sticking me in the nuthouse and never visiting me." But she sat down anyway. Raj had his list on top of her chart, and although it would be easy to check off "anger," "rage," "hostility," and every other synonym for being royally pissed off at the world, Claudia had never exhibited any of the other emotions on the page, except perhaps self-pity. She perfectly accepted the role of a martyred victim married to a cheating son of a bitch, month in and month out.

"How do you feel this morning?" asked Joanie.

"How do *you* feel, honey?" Claudia shot back. "Like jumping into another doctor's pants?"

Joanie didn't blush. "Not this minute," she said coolly. "I'm taking the day off."

Good one, Raj thought. He decided to push the envelope immediately. "Does Joanie remind you of the kind of girls who jump into Stanley's pants?" Claudia's eyes widened, and she stuttered in her reply.

"Probably," she mumbled. "If he's lucky."

"I can imagine how you feel when one of those bitches gets her claws into him," said Raj, holding his breath. He didn't want to launch Claudia onto the familiar path of rage, yet he had to get some feeling out of her that wasn't isolated and buried beyond retrieval.

"I don't know," Claudia said, hesitating.

"Yes, you do," Raj encouraged. "It's midnight and you're turning off the lights around the house, knowing that Stanley isn't coming home until morning. Your mind forms pictures of him and some woman, no matter how hard you try to push them out of your mind. How do you feel?" There was silence as Claudia shifted in her chair, her eyes glancing out at the magnificent tree standing sentinel in a sea of beauty that meant nothing to her.

"Lonely, that's how she feels," Joanie said in a sharp voice. Her vehemence made Claudia almost jump. "That's how I feel, and when I see it coming, I hate the bitch just so I won't have to face how damn lonely it's going to be from now on without him."

Raj knew it was now or never. "Loneliness is a lot

worse than anger, because you can control anger. You have something to hold on to. When my first girlfriend dumped me for a basketball star and didn't even phone me first, I felt so bad I cried for days. I thought I would never have anybody again." Claudia's jaw literally fell open, the muscles working weakly in gasping tremors.

And then she began to cry. For the first time that anyone had ever seen, the huge beast of her grief and abandonment sprang out of the underbrush and caught her by surprise. Huge tears coursed down Claudia's face, and she made no effort to wipe them away. Her spasms were so powerful that she couldn't get words out, and after five minutes Raj and Joanie took her hands and held them until she could regain a little composure. Once she did, she looked crushed but also, in a strange way, joyous. The beast had pounced but it hadn't devoured her.

"Wasn't that a dilly?" she said, and unable to help themselves, the three of them burst out laughing. Claudia looked up at Raj, who did not disguise that he was on the verge of tears himself. If she hadn't been so overwhelmed, her jaw would have fallen open a second time to see that. "I don't cry in front of Stanley, not like that," she mumbled.

"Who taught you not to cry like that?" asked Raj, seizing the opening before it went away, buried under the tide of defenses that would roll back in after Claudia regrouped. Claudia looked startled and very frightened.

"Someone must have taught you that your tears were not worth anything, that others would never change no matter how much they hurt you. And that's why you swore you would never show him your sadness," said Raj. It was the right chord. Claudia burst into a new round of weeping, this time even more helpless and draining. Joanie nodded at Raj with newfound respect. Claudia had grown up with a prosperous, good-looking father who ran around on her mother. Eventually, after many affairs that his wife overlooked, the father never returned, and Claudia's mother plunged herself and her daughter into a lifetime fantasy of revenge. "It's not like Sherlock Holmes," Halverson had once told the group. "You can find out reasons for someone's suffering in five minutes. The hard part is getting them to go back and react to those reasons in a way that was never allowed before."

The rest of Claudia's hour was spent just sitting and not saying anything. She quivered a little once her convulsive crying ended. Raj was glad he had remembered to screen off this corner of the day room with a portable curtain from the medical wards. Even so, he could feel a rustling of curiosity beyond the screen. Another taboo violated, since patients aren't supposed to have any inkling of what went on in each other's sessions. Raj expected to catch more flak, yet for the moment, as he sat watching Claudia sniffle, he felt triumphant.

Afterward Joanie hugged him before going off to her duties. "You're a hammer," she said. "I think this is one oyster you smashed open, absolutely smashed."

"Let's hope," said Raj.

THE DAY AFTER his breakthrough session with Claudia, Raj was accepted to the residency program. As a reward, he took the first vacation he had had since joining the pavilion staff. On the back page of the travel section of the *Times* Molly found one of those cruises to nowhere, a three-day circle from New York up the coast and back again. Champagne, a cabin with a veranda, and huge midnight buffets with ice sculptures.

"I'll get cramps tomorrow. My understudy will die of gratitude," said Molly.

"It will be worth every penny. I didn't really want that condo anyway," Raj joked, knowing that he was running away from the possible shock waves his new approach might cause on the ward. Someone was bound to call Mrs. Klemper's sudden improvement a "temporary transference cure"—meaning that she felt better because she'd fallen in love with her doctor—and they all knew those cures didn't last. Raj wanted to feel like a miracle worker for three whole days.

After deciding for certain to sail away together, Raj made love to Molly. This time, too, was different. Raj was more aware than ever of her skin, the supple-ness of her movement beneath him, but now she was rising to meet him. Dark waters were being left behind as she rose. The dig of her sharp fingernails into his chest excited him more than before, when he had felt the pain first and had to work past it. He allowed Molly to be as abandoned as she wanted to be. She didn't say, "Let's do this my way, completely," yet she led the way.

Then she sank out of sight again, careless that he was even there. Without knowing that he had done it, Raj let her go. He cut the rope that had desperately kept her with him at every moment, as if she were the mother and he the anxious child, and in throwing her to free-dom, he didn't lose her but found something new—a place where the vastness embraced them both, saying, "You are not he and she anymore. Now you are *this.*"

They still felt entwined when they finally boarded the fancy white ship, which had three swimming pools and Las Vegas dining rooms tiered six stories up a glassed-in atrium. The trip was gaudy and bleak at the same time. Everyone but them looked as old as the longest-term schizophrenic on the ward. An old lady with emphysema and a portable oxygen tank sat at their table and said, with sweet apology in her voice, "I hope you don't mind. I don't talk much, but I still eat." The weather was typical of the North Atlantic in the fall, a sea of asphalt gray tossed under a shroud of fog. The bright outline of the Maine coast would break into view with its shocking orange foliage, only to be stolen back by the mist a moment later.

Everything, including the oxygen tank on wheels, seemed charmed. The wheezing old lady ate slowly and said very little. Raj wanted to lean over the nightly dose of lobster bisque and tell her she would be all right, but he had no right to draw her into his optimistic trance. It would only be false hope.

On the second day out she suddenly stood up, gathering her napkin and silverware in a bundle. "It's not good for me to hang around too many honeymooners. I'm an old maid," she announced. "I live in a big, empty white house my father left me in Vermont. He ran the last tannery in town. You probably don't know what that is."

"We're not on a honeymoon," said Raj.

The old lady looked dubious. "I can always tell," she said.

Molly changed the subject. "So you come on these cruises fairly often?"

"About five times a year. When my house gets to be too big and empty." The old spinster was still preparing to leave.

"That many? Then you're married to the sea, in a way," Raj offered hopefully.

"That's very poetic, but poetry doesn't cheer me up," she said. "I need to find people who complain a lot, people I don't know. That usually works. And then when I get back home I can forget all about them." She was already shuffling away, or they would have told her that she didn't really need to haul silverware to her next table.

"How strange," Molly said. Raj had images of the old lady lying in her stateroom, gaunt and gasping for breath, her lungs made worse by the cold damp air. He wondered if no one had ever loved her or if she was the remnant of someone's affections from long ago, a suitor who had enough common sense to woo the daughter of the richest man in a small town, no matter how tart she was.

"I imagine she's always been alone," said Molly. "She feels like it."

"She feels unlovable?" asked Raj.

"Not that. People don't find love because they're lovable."

"Why do they?"

"You love the people you've promised to love. Then when you find them, you keep the promise. She never promised anyone." As sad as her final words sounded, Molly didn't look perturbed.

"So she chose to be alone, and everybody in the world has respected that for seventy years?" Raj asked. Molly's notions intrigued him, but they still made him nervous.

"More or less. If we haven't made promises to people, they don't notice us; they don't attach," said Molly.

"So you think some people deliberately turn their backs on being loved?" said Raj.

"Why not? If love was automatic or forced on us, it wouldn't be love, would it? I'm not saying she made the right decision. Who really knows? If she didn't want to promise herself to someone, that's her right. She'll have more chances in her next life."

Raj wanted to ask when and where people made these promises. How did they pick each other out? What about disastrous love affairs or marriages that end cold and passionless? But Raj didn't ask these questions. He wanted to believe that Molly was describing a promise she had made to him.

A few hours before they reached port, the ship left the open sea and pulled into protected waters off Long Island. From the deck, they saw white sails and the hard glint of sunlight off the waves. The wind was still cold, and they huddled together by the railing. Raj found that his curiosity wasn't satisfied.

"Are some promises forever?" he asked.

"Maybe," Molly said slowly, as if she took the question very seriously. "Maybe a promise can be forever. None of us can say, can we? We haven't lived forever. We'd have to consider boredom and fatigue. People wear out. It would be pretty horrible to buy one pair of shoes with a lifetime guarantee."

"Not for a man, it wouldn't."

"I haven't said it right," she went on. "A promise isn't a contract with your name at the bottom or a binding agreement, but a different kind of thing. It lasts as long as it keeps your soul alive."

"And that's us," said Raj. "The way we are now."

Without answering Molly kissed him, then took her long shawl and threw it over both their shoulders. Raj accepted this. He wanted to believe the signs in their sex and their closeness outside of sex. He wanted love to have no future but the same intense present that never ends.

The ship docked late, and Raj was back on call

almost as soon as they disembarked. At the pavilion word had spread about Claudia's dramatic improvement. A new respect showed in people's eyes—those few he met on duty. Habib said, "Awesome," and let it go at that. Joanie dropped her flirtatiousness with the interns, which in its way was a bigger sign than stopping Mrs. Klemper from throwing coffee cans. Despite the usual flare-ups in the night, Raj felt good; he had returned to a peaceable kingdom.

The only ripple of disturbance came a few days later when Molly left a note on his door that said, "Call me." Raj dialed her number, wondering why she didn't just leave a message on the machine. But it was okay, sort of.

"I need to fly to California tomorrow," she said. "It's a thing in L.A. I didn't want to tell you about it until I knew for certain."

"Do you want to tell me now?" he asked. There was a pause at the other end.

"Please don't push on this, Raj, I have a headache and I don't want to argue. It's something I have to do, that's all." Molly sounded matter-of-fact, nothing mysterious or tense. She was simply asking Raj to let it go, so he did. She sounded grateful that "the thing in L.A." didn't turn into an issue, although he was very close to making it one.

"Just call me when you get to the airport, and the

moment you land. So I won't worry," Raj said. Their schedules made it impossible for him to take her to Kennedy.

He barely registered when night became the next day. The emergency room was a zoo, careening from dead quiet to all-out trauma care in five minutes. Raj was bent over a bleeding woman who had been hit-and-run on Amsterdam Avenue. A medical student was on the other side of the table pulling glass shards out of her skin. Raj had been called in on a consult because the woman was delusional. She saw angels in the ER.

"Are they here right now?" Raj asked.

"Keep away the wrath," the woman moaned. She could barely talk coherently because of the pain. The wall phone started ringing. "I think you should give her another injection of morphine or Demerol or whatever you gave her," Raj told the medical student. "Otherwise she won't be able to make any sense." He suspected the delusions were induced by shock and pain, not by mental derangement.

"I can't overdose her. The glass is everywhere," the medical student grumbled. The phone kept ringing, so Raj picked it up.

"I'm not asking you to overdose her," he said. The woman was screeching so loudly by now that he could barely hear what was being said on the other end.

"What? Who's dead?" The words he was hearing made no sense. "Is she a patient of mine?" The information was repeated. "All right, I'll be right there," Raj replied. The unbelievability of the news forced him not to comprehend, in the same way no one would comprehend the actual end of the world. "Thank you for calling."

After hanging up the phone, Raj took three steps back toward the table where the woman was now begging the angels to let her die. "Hold still, not much more to go," said the medical student. Raj froze, and some part of his brain began to absorb the news. The look on his face made the woman stop screaming.

"We found your name in her purse, but we're also calling the next of kin. Mary Mahoney. You know her? There was an incident at the airport. She collapsed in the ticket line, and EMS got her into an ambulance right away. But they were too late. She was DOA. The dispatcher says you can go to Bellevue if you want to see her. I'm sorry."

It didn't matter if the next three days went forward in time or backward, or if they stood still. A sheet of lead dropped over Raj's senses, and nothing mattered except the same helpless wish he woke up to every morning, the wish that nothing had ended—not Molly, not him along with her, not what they made together.

People who loved him tried to gather him up in the gentle arms of their care. The other doctors talked about a rare sort of arrhythmia that can occur in young women otherwise immune to heart attacks. Had he noticed her being short of breath coming up the stairs? Even once could have been a sign, but who would have picked it out?

It didn't matter who anyone was or what they said. Love and death had stalked Raj with infinite cunning. And to what purpose? To annihilate him, or just to show him that the two sisters, one in front and the other a step behind, both had the same name?

Molly.

Part Two

The Lessons
of Love

7.

Love isn't something you feel. It is
something you become.

—Raj Rabban's journal

MOLLY WAS LAID out in the funeral chapel at six
in the evening, dressed in the black sheath that Raj had
brought over, and a pair of patent-leather high heels.
The mortician's assistant seemed to pause for a second
when Raj handed the clothes to her. He realized numbly
that women don't get buried in party clothes. It was the
first thing he had grabbed out of Molly's closet, his chest
still heaving uncontrollably.

"Can I see her?" Raj had mumbled. The mortician's

assistant shook her head. Now wouldn't be a good time, she had said.

The funeral home was only a few blocks away, but it sent a limo to pick him up. The chapel was hushed when Raj walked in. He was surprised to see Daddy-ji and Amma in the fourth row. Before Raj could bring himself to tell them, Maya had confided in his parents about the breakup. They had been devastated, yet when Raj began to reveal a few details about Molly, his parents had done their best to adjust. It was all to little avail. They mentioned her name so rarely that Raj had assumed they were blocking her out. He was deeply touched that they cared enough about his loss to attend the funeral.

Molly's mother and father, the Mahoneys, didn't recognize him. They had flown in from the Midwest and there was no other family to fill the first pew. Because he and Molly had kept their affair so quiet, Raj wasn't considered a member of the family or even close. Molly's parents looked as crushed as people who have sworn not to show anything can look. They sat stiffly, staring straight ahead. It must have been their choice to bring in a Catholic priest. Raj felt his father's body stiffen against the wooden pew when the Mass began. His mother, wearing a somber gray sari, looked more lost and vulnerable than he could ever remember.

In the animal kingdom, Raj thought, *woman is the only creature whose face can shatter someone's heart.* That was true of Molly, and it had once been true of his mother when she was young and beautiful. It was still true in a different way.

Raj's lack of sleep made the ceremony seem to go by in slow motion. Words buzzed in his ear making no sense. At the end he walked up to the casket. "I know you didn't bother to attend this little affair," he whispered. "Not your crowd."

He pulled out a crumpled silk gardenia from his pocket, some bit of fluff that had rolled under the bed after a party, and placed it on the casket. The polished curved top made the flower slide off onto the floor. Raj walked away without picking it up.

ANYTHING COULD HAVE happened over the next week. The shock was too much for Raj to be able to sleep at all. He stared blankly at the television until complete exhaustion made him doze off. Even then he had dreams that seemed to belong to someone else. In one of them the Mahoneys showed up at his door.

"Hello, Roger. You're in. I thought you would be," said Mr. Mahoney. "Getting over the little incident pretty quickly, are we?"

"No," said Raj, "we're not." Molly's father was holding something by his side, a small silver object that Raj couldn't identify.

"You didn't phone, Mr. Mahoney," Raj croaked, his throat suddenly gone dry.

"The line's busy. You found someone else to talk to already?" her father said.

"Jack is just a bit upset right now. I brought you a casserole," said Mrs. Mahoney. She held out a pan of lasagna wrapped in foil. It wafted steam and warm cheesy smells.

Molly's father began to raise what turned out to be a small gun and point its silver snub nose at Raj.

"I made it without meat. Indians eat their lasagna without meat, don't they?" Janice asked.

The gun went off without a sound. Except for the puff of blue burned powder, you would have thought it was a toy. Raj woke up with a jolt. He felt a single bead of cold sweat run from his armpit to the cotton band of his boxers. This told him that he was sitting up. Otherwise all was darkness except for the glow of the TV. He got to his feet, and just then the dog down the street started barking. Raj stepped toward the wall where the light switch was, but he stumbled over a stool that appeared from nowhere. His forehead thumped on the floor beneath the threadbare carpeting. It took a second before he regained his feet, and when he did, he was all adrenaline.

"All right!" he shouted at the top of his voice. It came out as a shriek. "Nobody else move!" Feeling his way, he made it to the switch and turned on the light. Part of his horror was pacified, but his body, unfed and ignored too long, began shuddering violently.

"You've got to stop this," he told himself. He threw on some clothes and ran out the door.

After a meal and a drink, Raj showed up at the hospital around eleven. "I want my shift back," he announced to Clarence, who looked up with surprise. "No one should have to carry me. I'm okay without sleep. Don't ask me how. Have they ever done any studies on that?"

Clarence didn't reach for the schedule. "You're already covered this week," he said in a kind tone. "Go home and try to pull yourself together."

"I've been home, and I should be here," Raj insisted. "I need to be grounded."

Clarence lifted an eyebrow. "It's not all that real around here, you know," he said.

"Compared to what?"

There was a sudden plea in Raj's voice. "I don't feel

like I have any chances left outside of here. I'll just float away and not come back. I'll—Christ, I don't know. I could go somewhere I'll never return from."

"You know this?" Clarence asked. "Or are you just afraid of it?"

"I can't tell," said Raj.

"I see. Maybe you've been thinking that Molly's not dead?"

Raj was stunned. Clarence had spent thirty-six hours on shift, and thick tufts of black hair stuck out from his head at odd angles. Zoned or not, there was a sharp look behind his glasses.

"Don't be surprised to hear her voice or see her in a crowd," Clarence went on. "Open-heart patients see little green men from Mars climbing up their legs in the recovery room, but then I'd say you aren't in shock."

"Why not?"

"You found me. People in shock are more disoriented. Do you think you're in shock?"

"I—" Raj was at a loss for a reply. Death had touched an unfamiliar place inside him and he didn't know how to react. Every minute since the news, he'd felt it like a cold claw in his heart. Clarence waited. He wasn't going to act surprised by anything Raj said, but he wasn't going soft. Truth was kindness now.

Raj said, "I didn't want to go to the funeral."

"Because then it would be harder to keep your magical secret, that she's not really dead. Is she being cremated?" asked Clarence. Raj nodded. The question seemed like a horrible violation. It brought his mind to an image he couldn't bear to see for more than a fraction of a second—a beautiful body in flames.

"Then whose ashes will be coming home?" said Clarence. "I'd like you to tell me."

"I don't know. Indian families don't bring ashes home. It's bad luck," Raj mumbled.

"You're evading the question."

Raj felt his throat grow tight, and he couldn't reply. Clarence was satisfied, though. "You seem normal to me. This kind of grief is the toughest thing you'll ever go through. You might not cry for a while. Not the deep cathartic crying that you'll need. It hits at odd moments. Mentioning her ashes almost did it just now." Raj nodded.

Clarence thought for a second and said, "Congenital brain aneurysm."

"What?" said Raj.

"Almost no one diagnoses it until it ruptures. Just a possible. Did your girlfriend show any symptoms?"

"She had a headache and then she was gone," said Raj.

Clarence nodded. "In your position I would want to know every detail. Maybe your mind doesn't work that way." Clarence knew it did, and in time the facts would be consoling.

Raj looked around at the green-tiled room and the harsh, flickering fluorescent lights. "What do I do if she comes back?"

"If? She will. It's a natural part of grieving."

"But what should I do?"

"Talk to her, that's my advice. You're not going to do yourself any good trying to deny this experience or pushing it away. Try to feel your way through, little by little. Do whatever it takes."

Raj managed a sad smile. "Is this why they call psychiatry bullshit?" he said.

"Just let the psych part of your mind shut down," said Clarence. "You'll never be your own shrink. No one is. And in case it needs to be said, I am very, very sorry for your loss."

"Thanks," said Raj. The imaginary hand that had been squeezing his chest began to relax.

NOVEMBER BROUGHT EARLY snow, the kind that stayed on the ground just long enough to get dirty. Raj kept away from patients for two more weeks. The worst ones didn't notice that he had been gone, the rest shot hurt looks in his direction. It helped that psychiatry is a passive profession. All Raj needed to do was listen, or seem to. Since almost everyone on the ward wanted not to face their problems, it was fine with them if he drifted in and out. In the hallways nurses ducked their heads and murmured, "I'm so sorry." Raj put one foot ahead of the other, feeling as empty and bleached as a bone.

Almost a week passed before he remembered Sasha Blum. He reached for the phone. Two rings, three, four. There was no answer and no machine. Raj checked her chart again to make sure the number was right. When the second call produced nothing, he phoned Maya.

"Hello?"

"It's Raj. I hope you don't mind me calling like this."

"What is it?" Maya sounded neutral; there was no reason to think she would have heard about Molly's death.

Raj said, "I can't seem to reach Sasha, and I was wondering if you've seen her." Hearing Maya's voice shook him. She was close to the place inside him where Raj felt blame and remorse. He struggled to sound objective. "I see two follow-up blood tests on Sasha's charts but no more after that. They're important," he said.

"I know that." There was a pause as Maya thought

about something. "The last time I saw her was before Thanksgiving break," she said.

"But not since then?"

Worry entered Maya's voice. "No. I went over to the dorms a few days ago, but Sasha didn't answer her door. Maybe you should come with me this time. She might need a doctor."

"I'm on duty here for a while," said Raj, hesitating. He doubted he could control his emotions once he set eyes on Maya. Just being on the phone had required him to breathe in deep, even breaths.

"I don't have a good feeling about this," said Maya. "She could be wandering again."

"Okay, I'll meet you there. Just give me an hour," Raj said.

By the time he arrived at the dorms, Maya was waiting. She met him at street level in jeans and a gray NYU sweatshirt, acting friendly but removed. They didn't speak on the way up to the second floor. The hallway was littered with skateboards, old laundry, and an abandoned grocery cart. Maya produced a key from her purse and unlocked the door when Sasha didn't answer.

Raj had never seen a dorm room quite like Sasha's. There was an eerie order and everything was immaculate, the bed perfectly made up with a white teddy bear on the pillow. Some loose change lying on the dresser had even been arranged in neat rows.

"She must be pretending very hard this time," said Maya. "Look."

She pointed to the one disturbing note in the room, and it was very disturbing. A bag of potting soil had been dumped onto the floor and the dirt piled up into a cone. Out of it stuck a dead geranium, a china cat, and two candy bars. These offerings to some unknown god had been regularly watered, to judge by the plastic garden can that stood beside the dirt mound. Brown stains had seeped into the carpet, forming a dark ring.

Raj walked over to the window. There was no ledge, or he might have expected to find Sasha crouching on it, shivering and far from reality.

"So where would she be likely to go?" he asked. "To her parents?"

"I have a number, but I doubt it," Maya said. "They seem to be the kind who are happy to dump her here."

"That's one way to cope with guilt," said Raj grimly. "Did Sasha ever tell you where she wanders?"

"No."

In the dresser they found empty bottles of medication but no full ones. The last refill appeared to be September.

"I feel so horrible about this," mourned Maya. "I told

you I would bring her to the clinic, but she kept saying she had taken care of it. I should have caught on."

"Why?" said Raj. "If she wanted to push you away, that was her choice. You shouldn't blame yourself. The question is what to do next." Raj didn't put his heart into his words. He himself felt the urge to save Sasha that had been so strong in the hospital.

Maya thought of something. "There's always Barry," she said. "He's only a few flights up."

She led the way down the hall and up the stairwell. Raj was trying hard not to feel worse. Seeing Maya was so painful that he coped only by concentrating on their mission, but what he felt wasn't just guilt for what he had done to her. All along an inexplicable force had been in charge, the same force that had thrown Molly in front of him. It had arranged events so that they had fallen in love. But Raj had no idea what that force was. And there was no one to tell him, not Daddy-ji with his woebegone talks on karma, not Amma with her tearful sighs.

"When such awful things happen," Daddy-ji had told him after the funeral, "we must release them to God."

Raj was too numb at that moment to accuse a God who was so cruel that he allowed deep love to be murdered. Or an innocent like Maya to be abandoned without reason. Numbness wears off, though, and Raj swore to himself that the last person he would ever release Molly to was God.

Barry answered the door in a T-shirt and red pajama bottoms. A computer screen shone through the dim murk of his room. "I haven't seen her for a while," he mumbled. Dive bombers and explosions sounded in the background from the game he was playing.

"Can you help us figure out where she might be?" asked Maya.

"Naw, but if you see her, tell her it's cool to call me again." Barry looked at them as though he were a recently awakened raccoon. "I gotta get back to my studies now."

"I don't think you get it. This isn't a casual inquiry," Raj interrupted, using a tone that would keep the door from being shut in their face. "Sasha's sick. She needs her medication or else it could be very serious." Barry hung his head. Whatever he denied to himself about Sasha, he wasn't happy to see her doctor show up.

"No comment? Then let me ask you something," said Raj. "How much do you like sex?"

Barry was suddenly flushed and a lot more nervous. "Sleeping with someone isn't like going to the video store and renting a tape," said Raj. "Do you care about her at all?"

Barry looked mournful. "I, like, hit on her just the once, and she started hanging on to me. I told her she should get a life. Maybe that set her off. I dunno."

"That's not good enough," said Raj sharply. The boy looked startled. He turned back into his room and returned with a scrap of paper.

"There's this place she wanted me to go to. She met some people there, but I wouldn't go with her," he said, handing the scrawled address to Raj. "She freaks me out enough by herself." Whatever he was feeling, Barry had gotten up the nerve to shut the door this time, leaving behind the muffled sounds of World War III. Raj still wondered whether Barry or anyone Sasha's age had an interest in her beyond sex or whether some stranger might be the father of her child.

Raj was furious, but something else was happening. As he was leaving with Maya, they passed a Coca-Cola clock that had been hung in the dorm to add a note of holiday cheer. It was a big round replica of the kind that used to decorate gas stations, printed with a picture of Santa Claus holding up a green Coke bottle and grinning.

"I hope Barry didn't try to pass her along to his friends," Maya said. "She's so easy to take advantage of."

Raj heard her, but another sound intervened. Tick-tock. Without noticing, he hadn't heard that sound since Molly left. He hadn't smelled the bad coffee at the pavilion or felt the sadness of his patients. Now the gray blanket of grief was lifting, one small degree at a time.

"We'll find the father, and we'll find Sasha," Raj said.

It was hard parting with Maya and postponing the search, but Habib could cover Raj for only two hours. When he got back onto the floor, Raj asked him, "How do I look?"

"Like a zombie," Habib said. In other words, better. Raj wanted the world to come back, and yet part of him didn't. Like gravity, his grief had pulled him inward to the heart of himself, and it was there that he kept searching for Molly. Late at night he felt her presence, and in those moments of fierce hope, Raj sensed that dim forms were pressing up to a screen, trying to make him see.

Come through, he prayed, *I'm here.*

They only vanished, and he had to wait. Hopelessness could have set in, except for one episode, early in December. A new intern named Gus was at the weekly staff meeting. Gus had a football player's thick build and looked very earnest. He was laying it on thick, trying to impress Clarence.

"Benita is a sixty-four-year-old Hispanic woman

who came into the ER last week complaining of leg pains," Gus said. "Within a few hours she was unable to stand or walk. There seemed to be no physical reason. She began complaining that she couldn't feel her legs anymore and demanded to be admitted. The ER called for a consult, and I determined that Benita's sudden paralysis was classic hysterical conversion."

Clarence, who was irritated by jargon, interrupted. "How exactly did you make this determination?" he asked.

"When I asked her if anything had been happening in her life, Benita told me that her grown daughter had just died," said Gus, referring to his notes. "The daughter had been living in the same house and brought in most of the money that came in. Benita is a widow."

"And?" said Clarence, pretty much knowing what was coming.

Gus didn't like being interrupted, but he had a good close. "Benita can't face her deep fear of being alone, so she puts the blame on her legs. They prevent her from escaping her situation or facing up to it. Instead of being paralyzed by fear, it is much easier for her to be paralyzed by something physical."

Clarence nodded. "Comments?" he said.

"The old lady broke her hip," said Stratton, one of the second-year residents.

"What?"

"Gus missed it in the chart. They took an X ray, and the old lady has several badly healed fractures of the hip joint."

Looking appalled, Gus riffled through the chart, finally pulling out an X ray. He held it up to the light.

"Well?" said Clarence impatiently.

"Okay, it's there, and I should have looked closer," said Gus. "But these old traumas couldn't cause paralysis."

"They could cause enough pain for her not to want to walk, or to try very hard," Clarence pointed out.

Gus stammered, searching for a way out, but Raj wasn't listening. He had been slumped in his chair the whole time, and he kept seeing Sasha Blum with a cigarette in her gaunt, doll-like face. Every time the image returned, his stomach felt empty. This was the girl he had promised to bring out of darkness. That day on the ward, when he rode such a wave of idealism, seemed very far away.

"She doesn't even know what hit her."

Raj thought he was talking to himself, but Mona, seated next to him, jumped slightly.

"Who?" asked Clarence.

"This woman. Her daughter died, and she doesn't know what hit her. That's the real reason she's paralyzed." The others stared in his direction since he hadn't spoken up in meetings for a month. "Anything we tell her is just a story, isn't it?" said Raj.

"We're trying to find the right story," said Clarence.

"Then we've failed," Raj retorted. "I had someone very close to me die. Someone who was achingly beautiful. She existed, and then in one unbelievable stroke she was destroyed. What story do you want me to believe? I know the medical terms, but those explanations won't tell me where she's gone. Can any of you?"

Mona had placed her hand on his arm. "It's all right," she said softly. Raj was too blinded to read anybody else's reaction, whether of compassion or embarrassment. Clarence broke the awkward silence. "We all know how much you hurt," he said.

They were sensitive people, and they knew that Raj was struggling. Seeing their looks of helpless sympathy, he thought, *She was inside me. You can't tell me she's gone.* Clarence brought the topic back to Benita and advised Gus to write a scrip for painkillers with a note to admit her the next time she showed up, should the weakness in her legs get worse.

After such a gut-wrenching day, Raj went home and collapsed on the sofa. The dog down the street was barking again, incessantly, which kept him awake. There was a knock on the door. Raj opened it and saw Molly.

"Prove to me you're not going to cry," she said softly.

She wasn't wearing her black dress and shoes anymore but old jeans and one of his white shirts. *Oh my God*. Raj threw his arms around the figure before him, aching to feel Molly's body. He did. It was warm and real.

"Hey." She smiled. "I bruise."

Without holding her so tight, Raj kept his hands on either side of Molly's face. He brought his lips to her more gently, and she opened her mouth.

"Where have you been?" he asked.

"Inside you, just where you thought." Raj allowed her only to release these words before kissing her again. He needed this balm for his grief, nothing else.

When he could speak again, he said, "I couldn't live without you. It wasn't possible."

"You'll never have to live without me," Molly whispered. At that moment Raj believed her. His will had brought her back. His will and his need and his desire. The warmth of her skin proved it. He opened his mouth to tell her more, but Molly put her fingers to his lips.

"Please listen. I'm inside you."

Nothing changed in her voice; she was just as tender as before. Raj felt a stab of fear, though, as if his accusation against God, that he created love only to murder it, would be proved twice.

"It's not true," said Molly, reading his fear. "I can stay, as long as you need me. I've made a bargain."

With who? Raj heard himself think.

"I don't think you'd understand, not right now," she replied.

But I'll always need you.

"We'll let that be true for now," said Molly. She kissed him again, drawing him onto the sofa again, and they lay quietly until Raj had calmed down. It took calmness for him to know that he didn't have to worry about her coming back. It only proved the truth that she hadn't left. And what had Clarence told him? *If she speaks to you, listen.*

"I think I'm ready," said Raj.

Good.

8.

THE BLEAK DECEMBER sun woke Raj up late. He kept his eyes closed, listening. From down the street a delivery truck backfired; a moment later someone threw a beer bottle, glass smashing on concrete. But no breathing. Raj let his hand stray a fraction of an inch and stopped, refusing to feel the empty space beside him.

Dream. Ghost. Hallucination. Raj swept the words from his mind. He got up and stumbled toward the kitchen. As he drank the cold coffee left in the pot from yesterday, his brain slowly cleared. He heard Molly's words again.

I'm not going to go until I've told you everything. We loved, and we thought we were loving enough. But there's more.

She must have been inside him, because Raj felt her as close as his breath. He turned around, in case Molly had reappeared, but the kitchen, so cramped he could almost touch both walls, was empty. He could smell the stink of the broken radiator that Molly was so afraid would explode someday.

"You're going to teach me," he heard himself repeat.

Yes.

All right. The teaching, if he was supposed to receive it like a radio, didn't come. Whenever a patient had shown up at the pavilion hearing voices, it was a fight to get them to understand that the words being thrust into their minds, however bizarre, were their own. Raj had never considered anything else. He had not considered that merging is real. Two people can share one voice, and it doesn't matter who owns it.

Raj closed his eyes, and inside him Molly said, *We were on the brink, both of us. Something incredible was going to reveal itself.*

Then you died.

Don't ask me about that. Concentrate on this: I know now what we were going to experience. It's still here.

Be specific.

You are going to be called out.

Raj remembered this phrase, which was the closest Molly had ever come to explaining herself. Being called out meant that a light shone on you and woke you up. You knew who you were and why you existed. His heart began to race.

This applies to me?

It applies to everyone. But right this minute, yes, it applies to you, the voice said. *Because you promised to love and you loved. You even said that love had called you out. Whatever happens, remember that one thing.* Something had shifted, and the voice wasn't Molly's anymore. No, it was hers but with greater—what? Strength. Reassurance. Some part of Raj was desperate to feel these qualities again. Her death had stripped him of hope; now she was offering it back.

How will I know when this is going to happen? You still haven't told me enough, he thought.

Listen, act, feel.

The voice stopped. Raj could have mistrusted everything at that moment. He took a shower, got dressed, made fresh coffee to take to the pavilion in place of the awful stuff that the machine dispensed. As he did all this, a part of him returned to familiar sensations, and they were welcome. The cold air stung his lungs; the pretzel from the vendor was doughy soft and warm. Each familiar thing wanted him to return. What was on the other side? A voice he trusted and a body he knew he had touched. Was that enough? One of Daddy-ji's old Indian poets once wrote, "Clasped in your dear arms, life and death were joined in me like a wedding vow." So that was it. If Molly had come back to keep her vow, so would he.

At work, Raj found the address that Barry had turned over so reluctantly. When he got free around five, Raj phoned Maya, who was relieved that Sasha hadn't been forgotten.

"It doesn't seem to matter when I call her. She's gone, and we have to find her," Maya said.

They shared a cab and the driver dropped them off on a seedy gutted block of Avenue B. "There's nothing here," he said. The dirty gray and brick buildings were mostly boarded up, some screened behind metal securi-ty curtains.

"I have a feeling we could start over there," said Maya, pointing. On the opposite corner was a small clutch of young Latino and black women in micromini skirts. "Come on."

Maya headed across the street without waiting for Raj to object. He followed as she walked up to the girls. "I'm looking for a friend," Maya said. "About your age.

She might have looked kind of lost. Her name is Sasha."

The question was greeted with suspicious silence for a second before one girl said, "She be here a coupla times, yeah."

"Lost, like you said," offered another.

"Was she working with you?" asked Raj. His question created a burst of harsh, disbelieving laughter.

"No way, honey."

One of the taller girls, who seemed to be a kind of leader, spoke up. "She was lonely, and we seen her come by here a few times. I don't know if she went home with no one, but I don't think so. You might look in there." She nodded toward a bar a few doors down. "That's your best bet."

"Thanks," said Raj, pulling Maya away.

"Why did you ask them that?" Maya asked in confusion.

"Because Sasha's pregnant. That's protected information, but she's going to show soon enough," said Raj.

Maya didn't seem shocked. Perhaps Sasha had confided in her when she first found out. "I wonder if Barry and his friends have been here. Maybe they saw her here and it gave them a reason to hit on her first, not the other way around," she said.

"It's grim either way. Let's try in here." Raj opened

the glass-and-iron door to the bar, which otherwise had no windows, and let Maya in. The interior was smoky and dense with gloom. They walked past a few thinly populated tables to the bar. The tough-looking barman didn't come toward them until Raj called for two beers.

"We're looking for a girl, and someone told us you might have seen her," said Raj.

The bartender scowled. "I don't see no girls."

"I don't mean a working girl. She's a college student, thin, dark hair, and she might talk to herself sometimes," Raj said.

The man considered this for a moment. "You from the islands?" he asked.

"No," said Raj.

"Then you best come back later, after we close. There's a few girls come by then, and the one you talkin' about might be with 'em." Raj and Maya left their beers behind and departed.

"What do you think?" she asked when they were back outside. The sun was almost set now, the blue fast seeping out of the sky as the temperature plummeted.

"It's worth a chance, I guess. But you shouldn't stay here. I can hang around," said Raj, feeling weary and not at all hopeful.

"But you'll call?" said Maya. "Should I file a missing persons report?"

"If you're not family, the police won't listen very seriously," said Raj. "You're being great about this. But I need to tell you something. Molly died. It happened about a month ago, very suddenly."

He didn't know what more to say or if his words had hurt Maya again.

Maya's first reaction seemed to be embarrassment, and then a tear slid down her cheek. "I saw it when you showed up at the dorm. I wondered if something else had made you feel so terrible or if it was me," she said. Raj felt numb, not knowing how to react to her. "I'm really sorry, Raj, I'm really sorry," Maya said.

The two stood at the vacant corner under the light. The clutch of girls had moved on. Raj's mind drifted. At that moment, he yearned for isolation and quiet. "I think I should go," said Maya. She waved down a passing cab, which stopped twenty feet away.

"You seem to be trying to raise the dead. It probably won't work," she said, starting to move away.

"What?" said Raj, astonished.

"Sasha. No one at the hospital believes there's anything to be done except drug her. I know how sick she is, and I know how quickly the system would let her slide down the tubes. You're either trying to be a saint or you're in over your head."

She ran for the taxi and got in without waiting for a

response. The cab's tires squealed on the black ice in the gutter, and she was gone.

The bar closed at two, which gave Raj six more hours at work. He found Claudia looking for him the moment he got back on the floor.

"Why weren't you here an hour ago?" she said. She couldn't help coming on strong and sour. Raj thought this might be a good sign. He had missed all their sessions for a month, and she wanted him to feel how much that hurt.

Raj said, "I went out to help somebody, another patient who is off her meds, and it took too long. I'm sorry." Claudia's face fell. She didn't expect an apology.

"Who was it?" she asked.

"Come on, you know that's over the line," said Raj.

"Being crazy isn't over the line enough?"

Claudia burst out laughing, and Raj let her in his office, giving an encouraging smile. "Do you know why the chicken crossed the road?" Claudia asked.

"No."

"Neither does he, but his therapist thinks it's probably about his penis."

When Raj kept wearing his smile, Claudia said, "That's better. You've been looking bummed lately."

"I know. How was your visit home?" he asked.

Claudia had taken a trip over the weekend to see if she could adapt to being with her husband again.

"Fine," she said.

"What does fine mean?"

Claudia shrugged. "A truce. That's pretty good, right? Stanley played some golf, and he took me out after. It was nice." She wasn't meeting Raj's eyes.

"That does sound nice," Raj agreed. "Nice for Stanley, at least. Did you talk about your problems together?"

Claudia shook her head. "Stanley says that when I come home it's one of our good times, and why should we spoil it by fighting?"

"Discussing how you really feel isn't fighting," Raj pointed out. "It's being honest."

"It upsets him too much," Claudia mumbled.

"Really? I would say it doesn't upset him at all. It inconveniences him. How do you feel about being his inconvenience?" Claudia stared out the small window that overlooked the parking lot. Nothing could be seen in the well of darkness outside. Raj waited for an answer, and when it didn't come, he said, "Can I be totally straight with you?" Claudia nodded weakly, not giving much of a yes, but enough so he could say what he wanted to.

"You're using this hospital as a revolving door. You know it, and I know it," said Raj. "What I don't know is if you want to quit."

"You think I like being miserable?"

"You like what comes with it."

"Which is what?" Claudia asked suspiciously.

Raj sat back. "You get sympathy. You get to shut out Stanley, who probably bores you to death and has for quite some time. You get to be right. You get to play the part of victim. And best of all you get to come here and have a lot of people pay attention to you when you're totally out of control. Sounds like a pretty great bargain to me."

He was only halfway through before Claudia was on her feet, her face racked with betrayal. "You little *pisher!*" she yelled. "Who gave you the right to talk to me like that!"

Raj stood up and came close enough to make her uncomfortable. "You did, in case you forgot." He said this evenly, without aggression, and although his tone could be thought cruel, he tried to convey with his voice his desire to see someone, anyone, emerge from self-inflicted pain.

"Of all the horrible things that could have happened in your life," Raj said, "you have chosen to do most of them to yourself."

"Don't you believe it," said Claudia hotly. "I didn't send that bastard into someone else's bed. I didn't ask him to cheat and lie and treat me like a little nobody he can push around."

"Look at yourself right this minute," said Raj. "That's exactly what you've done. You married a guy who could be predicted by someone with half your IQ to cheat and lie, and you chose to fill your side of the equation. Didn't you?"

"No!" Claudia was beginning to cry.

"Leap over the wall," Raj said, raising his voice. "You're better than that. See the truth. It's not going to kill you, and you're dying anyway, so what the hell?"

Her eyes, streaming now, grew very large. "What are you saying?" Her voice was trembling.

Raj drew closer and put his hands on Claudia's shoulders. "You know what I'm saying. There's no wall but the one you built," he urged gently.

That's enough.

No one heard the words but Raj. He whirled around to see Molly standing by the door. "She isn't hearing you," she said.

Raj turned back. Claudia was gasping for air, her eyes filled with alarm.

"You were going to treat her with love, remember?" said Molly. "That's not what you're doing."

Raj couldn't deny it. Claudia was pacing now. She was wiping her eyes with both fists. "You're trying to kill me," she gasped weakly. Strands of sticky gray hair stuck to her face. "If I listened to you, I'd be dead."

"She's right," said Molly.

No, she isn't!

Raj had to trust that Claudia didn't see anyone else in the room. For a second, her eyes went to the corner where Raj had stared, but they came back immediately.

"Try to calm down," Raj said.

"How can you expect her to calm down?" said Molly. "She feels attacked."

At that moment two things happened. Taking a deep breath, Claudia swung hard at Raj, hitting him in the face, while at the same time Joanie appeared in the open door.

"You don't love me!" Claudia shouted.

"What's going on?" said Joanie, who looked stunned.

No one paid any attention to her. Claudia collapsed into Raj's arms, heavy with weeping. "I thought you loved me," she blubbered.

"Don't," said Raj, struggling to peel her off. "You're not helping yourself this way."

"I don't care!" wailed Claudia. "I think about you, and I've missed you so much." She tried to embrace him again, but Joanie stepped in. She was beginning to look amused.

"Calm down, I'm here now," Joanie said, as much for Raj's benefit as the patient's.

"We don't want you here. Get out!" shouted Claudia. "And get your hands off me!"

She made another lunge at Raj, and one of her breasts fell out of her robe. Seeing the look on Raj's face, Claudia froze. "Oh my God," she exclaimed, putting a hand over her mouth. "You hate me."

"No, I don't. This is just a misunderstanding," said Raj.

"I'll say," Joanie added, more amused by the minute.

"You think I'm a pathetic old woman you can just lead on," said Claudia. "How could you do that?" She fought between being stricken and being outraged. "Don't you have any decency?"

"Please, sit down and compose yourself," said Raj. "I'll try to explain things to you."

"Things? *I don't want to be a thing anymore!*" cried Claudia. She swung back and would have landed another slap on Raj's face if Joanie hadn't caught her arms and thrown her off kilter.

"Hey!" Joanie shouted. "I'm pulling you out of here, right now."

"No!"

In her turmoil, Claudia was surprisingly strong. She made a grab at Joanie's hair but not before Joanie caught and held her wrists.

"Any more of this and I'll call for restraints," Joanie warned.

Raj shook his head. "That's not necessary. It's going to be okay," he said. He turned to Claudia. "Isn't it?"

She was already running out of steam, and something had shifted inside her. Despite her upset, Claudia sensed what had really happened. The very words she'd needed to scream for years—*I don't want to be a thing anymore*—had come out of her mouth, maybe not directed at the right person, but at least they were out. Raj looked around. Molly was still there.

"What she calls love is her need. It's real," Molly said. "If you deny her need, all she'll be left with is fear."

What do you expect me to do? Raj thought.

"Give her what she needs. That's all love can do sometimes. Show her that she isn't a nobody. That's her greatest fear. Forget how she looks or how she sounds. You have a child here."

Raj took a deep breath. "Leave us alone, please," he told Joanie.

She looked skeptical. "Because you're doing such a bang-up job alone?"

Claudia laughed harshly. "Good one," she said, her body relaxing. She shoved the wandering breast back into place.

Joanie said, "Okay, I'll come back in a while." She gave Claudia the eye. "You've had your rampage for the day. Got that?"

After Joanie left the room, Raj handed Claudia a Kleenex. "Your prize," he said.

"Like I deserve one," Claudia snuffled. She blew her nose and took a huge gulp of a sigh. "I made a damn fool of myself."

"Yeah, she did," remarked Molly. "But lucky for her, she made a damn fool of herself at just the right time."

Listening, Raj said, "I mean it when I congratulate you, Claudia."

She grinned ruefully. "I really thought today was the day I would make my play. I've been thinking about it so much."

"I'm glad you did. Really. Of course, this is one hell of a way to get better," said Raj. "But you stopped hiding behind your issues, and that means those issues don't have to run you anymore." Claudia nodded, absorbing what he said as much as she could.

Standing in the corner, Molly said, "She wasn't just fantasizing about you. She thinks that love is protection. Millions of people are like that. You need to speak on that level."

All right.

"Claudia, I want you to know that you're taken care of," said Raj. "You don't have to put up with Stanley just because he provides. Is that how your marriage started?"

Claudia nodded. She was listening closely.

"Someone else is watching over you," said Molly. "Tell her."

As she said these words, Raj felt their full meaning. Claudia's issue was survival. She could not believe that she was anything but a small, isolated creature. This had created so much fear that she would pay any price for someone stronger who would take care of her. But it was a bad bargain, because in giving her power to a protector, none was left for herself. All her tantrums were just shows of power with no direction behind them.

"I want you to hear me," Raj said to her. "Stanley's not going to save you. It's not in his interests anymore. He has you where he wants you, and now he knows he can get away with murder."

There was no look of shock on Claudia's face. She waited for the next thing Raj would say.

"See, she's not frightened," said Molly. "She's finally sick enough of her illusions to let them go. No one changes until that moment comes."

Now what? thought Raj.

"If you really want to show love, what everyone needs first is reassurance. They need to know that they're safe."

"What you need to do," Raj said to Claudia, "is to find a place without Stanley. Go there, and let your fear come up. We take care of you here, but only when you keep acting crazy. But you're still afraid a lot anyway, aren't you?"

Claudia nodded.

"You can be your own protector," said Raj. "It's not physical; it's something you find inside. That's your journey. If you take the first step, things will change. Your fear is being summoned to fill an empty place, but that's not real. You aren't empty at all. You've simply lost contact with that part of yourself that stands for strength."

"Tell her that this is what God wants for her," said Molly.

Raj felt his own doubt begin to rise, but when he looked at Claudia, the first patient who had the courage to plead for his love, he had to give her the whole truth, as Molly was giving it to him.

"God wants you to make this journey," said Raj.

"Your fear and emptiness are not part of his plan. Old hurts and old wounds created them. If you could see yourself through God's eyes, you would see that you are completely loved and completely protected. Reach out for your strength, and you'll never feel unprotected again."

There was no distance between the healer and the healed at that moment. Raj had received as much from Molly's teaching as he had given. *Someone is watching. Someone cares. You are always protected.* Molly had found this out, and now Raj could speak it.

For her part, Claudia had been transformed—it was a moment of clarity that she had never experienced before, and she could see far ahead. "God, I really do love you," she exclaimed.

"I love you, too," said Raj. He didn't have to look behind him to know that Molly was gone.

It was one a.m. when Raj made his way back to Avenue B. He decided not to wait in the bar but to walk the streets until two. Riding over on the bus, he had tried to bring Molly back again but without success. Now he had many more questions than answers. Was she real? Clarence had told Raj to talk to her, yes, but Clarence would have called this a projection caused by grief. Projections don't know what Molly seemed to know. Or do they? Raj hadn't felt that she was manipulating him from beyond. Instead Molly had expressed things Raj already knew in some deep part of himself yet couldn't access. Maybe that is what lovers mean when they claim that their beloved is inside them. Their merging erases separation; it opens up the self in some remarkable way. This certainly appeared to be true for him. Raj felt elated, as if he could see Molly and at the same time be in her world. Yet he had no idea what that world really was. A secret world to which Molly held the key? Only she could tell him, and for now she was staying away.

For half an hour Raj watched the stragglers leaving from across the street. The last to come out was the bartender. He didn't look directly at Raj if he even noticed him. Raj crossed the street and opened the iron-and-glass door. The bar was empty except for two cleaning women in the corner and a third sitting against the bar smoking a cigarette. She wore a coral necklace and a loud tropical blouse that looked out of place for the verge of winter.

Raj approached and said, "I'm looking for a girl."

"She's with me," the woman said calmly.

"So you know Sasha? I don't see her here," said Raj.

"No. This is no place for her." With his eyes adjusted,

Raj saw that she was lightly colored, perhaps Creole—an island lilt to her voice gave it away. "I'm keeping her safe," she said.

"That's not good enough," Raj replied. "I am her doctor and she needs her medication."

"These?" She held up a pill bottle and rattled it. "I've been watching them. I am Serena. If you want to see her, wait a while. I'll take you."

"Okay." Raj was relieved to find that the worst wasn't true. He had vaguely worried that Sasha was hiding in the bathroom and wouldn't come out.

Serena looked over at the other two women, who had stopped wiping off the bar to stare at the exchange. "Dolls, this is just for me and him," she said, and they went back to work. She turned back to Raj. "I didn't think you'd be so interesting," she said.

"What's interesting about me?" asked Raj.

"Well, when I first feel you, it isn't so good. You have been through a lot of pain and sorrow." The woman eyed him like a cat, at once detached and alert, more alert than anyone Raj had ever seen.

"I'm sure it shows," said Raj uncomfortably.

"But that's not everything," said Serena. "There are other moves on the board for you. After despair comes something that could be beautiful. And powerful at the same time."

"I hope so," said Raj, feeling pulled by Serena's ability to see him but wary at the same time. She sensed this.

"Sasha tells me you treat people. That's not what I do," she said.

"What would you say you do?" asked Raj, looking at the mop and bucket resting against the bar. Serena laughed.

"Not this, honey," she said. "I run a cleaning service so poor girls can have work. The one who usually supervises was sick tonight."

"Then you do something else?" said Raj.

"I could tell you the name Molly and surprise you very much," said Serena.

Raj jumped. "You got her name. You're some kind of reader?" he said.

"She's with you. It's not a secret, though maybe most people would say we can't know such things. But I think you and I can be more honest. You think so, too?" She waited for his answer, and both the qualities Raj had noticed were there. Serena seemed detached about being able to see or sense Molly's presence, while at the same time she was extremely alert to everything.

"Yes, we can be honest," said Raj. "If you can't already tell, I've been talking to Molly."

"Do you think she's a ghost?" asked Serena.

"I don't know. If I came up with an answer, I'm not sure I would trust it."

"I'd say you're fairly well caught," said Serena.

"Why do you say that?" asked Raj.

"For the same reason that a crazy person is caught. You know about crazy people, yes?"

"A little."

"They walk around in two worlds, theirs and the real one. Half the time they are lost on fantastic, terrifying journeys; half the time they're trying to buy cereal and toilet paper like normal people. It's exhausting, and it's pointless. No one can live in two worlds, so they gradually lose the battle. They must tip one way or the other. Either madness claims them or reality does. Then the issue is settled. The fight is done for good."

"And you think I'm like that?" asked Raj.

"Don't play games. When you walk through a crowd, you can see who the crazy ones are immediately. No one else is having a hard time buying cereal and toilet paper. They twitch, they shiver, they have a lost look that makes everyone else walk around them. When I look at you, I see the same thing, only you're not crazy. So the two worlds you live in are different." Having finished her cigarette, Serena took a bandanna out of her jeans and wrapped it around her dark, short-cropped hair. She went over to the other two cleaning women and started working with her mop and bucket.

"You know what?" Raj called across the room. "I was someone's hero today. I let a madwoman jump me, and because of that she hit the wall a lot faster than if I had let her drift into it. Funny thing, huh?"

"Molly thinks so," Serena called back, "but then, she's got a better seat now." Serena bent her back and worked hard, paying no attention to Raj.

She was giving him time to think. The woman's stone confidence shook Raj and made him want to turn to her. She was not anyone's fantasy of a mother figure—large, enveloping, kind. Serena was almost bony, and her accent could be as sharp as flint when she was making a point. The least comforting thing about her was that she was right about him. He was living in two worlds, and it probably was inevitable that he would tip one way or the other.

9.

Y OU THINK THESE things don't happen?" said Serena. "They do."

Raj was lying on the backseat of a brown Dodge Dart as the overhead street lamps blurred past. They had already dropped off the two cleaning women and were headed toward Queens.

"So you think I'm talking to someone who's real?" asked Raj.

"In my opinion, yes. But then, I have the gift of imagination," said Serena, laughing.

"It took more than imagination for you to see me that way," said Raj. "How did you know?"

"Everybody knows," said Serena. "But they pretend not to. It's more respectable that way. You can keep secrets that way."

"And you don't believe in secrets?" said Raj.

"That's right, I don't," said Serena. "I'll tell you about me if you're curious. I grew up in Dominica, very poor, beyond what you'd imagine as poor. I played in a hole in the ground. What made me happy was the freedom of having nothing. My mother took care of five younger children and could barely take a breath. Without meaning to, she gave me the gift of total solitude to go along with total poverty.

"One day when I was five I ran away from church and got beaten for it. I thought the eyes of the crucified Jesus were following me, and I got scared. So I ran home and hid in my mud hole, looking up at the sky. After the beating I went back there and hid all night, with just a candle. After a while, the candle burned out. When you are five, it's easy to forget that your house is only a few yards away through the trees. Ordinary birds and animals sounded fearsome at night. A dog's howl seemed to come from hell.

"The instant the candle went out, I wanted to scream, but instead of complete darkness, I was surrounded by figures and faces. They didn't look like the angels carved on either side of the altar in church, although those were the only extraordinary things I had ever seen besides lightning and a thousand blue parrots. The figures stayed very still, and they stood out in the dark like the flame of the candle but not nearly as bright."

Serena stopped, just at the point that Raj thought she would tell him more. He waited. She turned away from the drive by the river and seemed engrossed in finding the right exit. Raj wasn't sure what was happening except that a "No Turning Back" sign seemed to flash in his head.

"So who were they?" he asked. Then suddenly he knew. They were like the dim forms that had been pressing up against the screen, leaving him clues, trying to make him see. Only now one had made it through.

"Is Molly like that?" he asked.

"For you, yes," said Serena. "But even more alive, even more present. She's giving you an opening. It's like those scenes on TV, where refugees are lined up at the border, women holding their children and the old men crying. Their homes are gone, and they have to cross, but they're afraid. They don't know what kind of new life awaits them." Serena's voice seemed to float toward him in the dark.

"It sounds dangerous," said Raj.

"Sometimes it is. But without the unknown, there is no new life at all."

Raj's confusion had subsided. It was comforting in a way to be in no-man's-land. To tell the truth, Raj had spent so much time with sad people, damaged people, and crazy people that he was all too familiar with where they wound up and knew almost nothing about the other direction. Serena seemed to know a great deal about the invisible road he was on.

"So I'm not the first?" he said.

Serena laughed. "You mean my first? No, honey, not by a long shot."

"And what will I break through to?" asked Raj.

"It's different for everyone," Serena said. "Some say there's a light. I've never seen it. All I've figured out is that once you get over the border, you'll know it, and then when you walk down the street and see someone else who's going there, it often stands out. It's silent and shared at the same time. But like I say, everyone's different. It's strange."

"I bet."

She gave him a sharp look in the rearview mirror. "You didn't think living was just the same old stuff, did you? One big weekend at the mall with nuclear weapons in the cornfield and wine with lunch. I expect you had some idea up to now, right?"

"Something like that," said Raj. "It all began with her. She was my one big clue."

"She's more than a clue. I think you're going to make it."

"You can tell that because I look so good?" said Raj, who was slowly adjusting to Serena's uncanny confidence. Looking up at the sodium arc lamps over the highway, he wondered if a Persian farmer at the time of Zoroaster had gazed up at the stars with the same sense of impending mystery, as if something lay behind them wanting to speak to him. Or perhaps his own ancestors had felt like this, somewhere deep in the past.

They pulled up to a brick bungalow on a nondescript street. It was too dark to make out any features, though a light was on behind some pale muslin curtains in the front. As Serena led him inside, Raj saw Sasha sitting curled up in an armchair before the all-knowing eye of the television.

"Hi," she said, not looking up. She was wearing pink pajamas; the raccoon mascara was gone.

"I brought this nice man home," said Serena, slipping off her shoes and throwing the bandanna onto the sofa before sitting down. "You feeling all right?"

Sasha nodded. She looked over at Raj with some anxiety in her eyes.

"I'm just here as a friend," Raj said. "We can talk about any other stuff later. Or we can just hang out."

This calmed her, and Raj was relieved. There was a long way to go to get Sasha out of the woods, but he had found her. Raj looked around. It was a house much like his parents', with thick walls from the post-war period and textured plaster. A cheap chandelier hung from the dining area at the end of the all-purpose living room and beyond that was a breakfast bar. Just like home minus the Shivas and the warm scent of curry.

"Do you live here alone?" he asked.

"Mostly," Serena replied. "The world comes calling."

"Like me," said Sasha. The room was quiet except for hushed violins emanating from an old movie. The shrink part of Raj's brain noticed that Sasha was free from rigidity or tremor. Her body lay softly in the chair; she seemed to know that the voices in the room belonged to real people. Raj wanted to ask her about morning sickness and any other indications of her pregnancy, but this wasn't the setting.

"I'm only here till seven-thirty, then I've got to get back," he said. "Maybe you should come with me. Maya wants to see you."

"All right," said Sasha, seemingly unconcerned.

Serena gestured him toward the kitchen. "I think staying here is better for her, at least for now," she said once they were parked on either side of the sink. The kitchen smelled of orange peels and dishes waiting to be washed. "We need to go on instinct here."

"What makes you say that?" asked Raj doubtfully.

"*It*," said Serena.

"What do you mean?"

"There's no other word I can use." Serena waved her arms as if to include everything around them. "*It* knows everything, arranges everything. I didn't accidentally find Sasha, and you didn't accidentally find me. *It* brought us together, the same way you and Molly were drawn to each other."

"I don't think we can compare the two," Raj said stiffly. He wondered if Serena's *It* was the same unknown force that had been guiding him.

"Your problem is that you want to keep one thing special, protected, sacred. That way you can still believe that Molly hasn't died. She has, even if she's back," said Serena. "Unless you learn all you can, you'll just be left with a memory when she stops coming to you. How different is that from anybody who's lost someone?"

Raj swallowed hard. This was cutting close to the

bone, yet he did have to face all possibilities, including the one that Molly would never be back.

Serena read his anxiety. "Your bargain with her isn't over. Not for you or for Molly," she said.

Raj felt agitated. Serena was right about him wanting to keep Molly special. The thought of stripping that away panicked him. "What if there is no bargain? What if I'm just desperately reaching?" he said.

"Then you'll live with grief. Next question."

That uncanny confidence again. Serena still seemed amused by him, which was annoying, but her attention was less cat-like. Raj had no doubt of her sincerity, and it was likely that Serena was a very positive influence on Sasha. Perhaps she had a gift for lessening confusion.

"I have to go now," Raj said. "You should still consider me Sasha's doctor for now. There's a lot of medical stuff that needs tending to, seriously. I guess that's it."

Serena touched his sleeve as he was about to walk away. "When you look at me now, you don't see what I've gone through. I'm just an ordinary woman who runs a cleaning service, and sometimes I hire people who are in trouble. But at least I can give you my map."

"You drew a map?"

"Not while I was going through the wringer, no. But afterwards I didn't want to forget the way. You won't want to, either."

She left and came back with a single piece of paper. On it Raj saw three words.

"Take it. They're important," Serena urged. She folded the paper and stuck it in his pocket. "Don't look so disappointed. Next time I'll try and shoot sparks from my tits, how's that?"

When Raj said good-bye in the living room, Sasha was asleep with drive-time chatter filling the TV. He hadn't gotten close enough to see if she was showing yet under her loose clothes. Down the street, once he found the right bus stop, Raj opened the piece of paper curiously.

It said, "Anything is possible."

THAT DAY RAJ was assigned to the outpatient clinic. The morning brought a rush of patients. A depressed woman was brought in because her grown children thought she had suicidal impulses—she had bought three boxes of rat poison after learning she was pregnant. This news came at age forty-one, two weeks after her husband announced he wanted a divorce. Another patient, an old man in his seventies, had spiraled into involutional psychosis on the third anniversary of his wife's death; he hid under the bed and said he was defending the trenches from German attack. A mother brought in her tearful teenage daughter, saying she was a rabid nymphomaniac—though it was fairly clear the girl was normal and the mother potentially disturbed.

It was weird trying to talk patients out of their fantasies while getting ready to dive deeper into his own strangeness. Raj hoped to see Molly again. When she didn't appear, he went inside and said, "Okay, we're doing this together. See through me. I'll speak for both of us." He had the sense that she understood and was with him.

To the woman with three boxes of rat poison he said, "I don't agree with your children. I don't think this is about killing yourself, is it?"

"How do you know?" the woman said, not agreeing or disagreeing.

"By the time you bought the first box, you had enough to do the job, but you kept buying more. Why is that?" Raj asked.

"I don't know. I just kept going back," she said.

"You didn't hide them that well, so let's say you liked the idea that someone would find them," Raj suggested. "You wanted the gesture to be dramatic. You wanted someone to notice you after years of being mistaken for wallpaper."

The woman stared back at Raj blankly. He hesitated, wondering if he was totally off base. Poison and suicide were a pretty natural supposition.

Don't doubt. You're almost there, he heard Molly say.

Raj asked the woman if she felt so neglected that she wanted to do away with herself. She said no. He asked if she had gotten pregnant on purpose. She said no again. He asked if she felt overwhelmed by her husband leaving her and the pregnancy both coming at once.

"I'm just depressed. Can't you give me something instead of asking me all these personal questions?" the woman said, growing impatient. Raj reached for his pad, resigned to giving her what she wanted, when he heard the voice inside him.

Tell her she's lying.

The woman was holding her hand out now, waiting for the prescription. Raj looked her directly in the eye. "I can't give these to you. You haven't been telling the truth," he said. Her eyes widened, and Raj had a flash. "You tricked your husband. He hasn't been able to touch you for years, but you told him that you wanted to have sex again, and often. You had the birth-control pills in plain sight, but you didn't take them. You wanted to get pregnant, and when it worked, he got so furious that he swore he'd leave."

Now her jaw had fallen open. "What are you saying? Are you accusing me?" she said, looking deeply shaken.

Tell her it's all right. Having the child was the right decision.

"No one's accusing you," said Raj gently. "Your motive was as human as it gets. You wanted a guarantee that you were loved. Isn't that what a baby can be trusted for? And what your husband couldn't be trusted for?"

Good.

Raj expected the woman to look stricken or to break down crying. But she smiled as if a deep reassurance had come to her. "I didn't think I had a right to bring a baby into the world for selfish reasons. It was all backfiring. Harry had started to hate me. You're saying it's all right?"

"Yes."

Watching the relief spreading over her face, Raj saw a pattern in what Molly was doing. She was connecting people back. Each of them, counting himself, had lost a connection. Their souls were muffled in layer after layer of hurt, self-judgment, and doubt. They operated out of anger and fear, because they didn't know there was anywhere else to go. With Molly's help, he was showing them—and showing himself—that they were not lost. If he couldn't reach them, Molly could.

The pattern continued this way. He told the woman with the nymphomaniac daughter to leave the room for a moment, and when she was gone Raj turned to the daughter.

"Don't be afraid," he said. "You're not the patient here."

"What do you mean?"

"Does your mother go to see a psychiatrist?" asked Raj. The girl didn't answer. "Families keep secrets when they shouldn't, out of shame, sometimes," said Raj.

"I hate the way she treats me!" the girl blurted out.

"So you go out every night, even when you have to sneak. Is that what gave your mother the idea that you're sleeping around?" Raj asked. The girl nodded miserably.

Tell her the boy won't solve anything. Jeffrey.

"I have a feeling there's a boy that you lean on, that you think will be the answer to your problems. He won't," said Raj.

"Jeff is good to me. She's a bitch," the girl said resentfully.

"But he's not your family, and you're both too young to start another one together," said Raj.

"What do you expect me to do? She thinks I'm a nympho already."

Give her courage.

"You're going to have to be brave. Your father won't play his part. His own mother was committed when he was a boy, and now he can't bear the thought of betraying your mom like that. So it's up to you. We'll be allies, you and me. You keep a quiet watch on her for a week, then call me here at the hospital. If your mom keeps acting like this, I want you to bring her back on your next visit. Then we'll try to find some medication for her," said Raj.

Perhaps because she was young or simply at her wit's end, the girl accepted this without a dramatic reaction. But as she was leaving, Raj noticed that her head wasn't hanging anymore, and she turned at the last minute to embrace him.

Only the shuddering old man fighting the Battle of the Bulge from under his bed was too terrified for Raj to reach. Raj wrote up a heavy dose of tranquilizers and scheduled a follow-up in a week.

At noon, still feeling as energized as if he'd had a full night's sleep, Raj picked up the phone to call Maya. Habib stuck his head in. "Lunch?" he said.

Raj was listening to the phone ring at the other end. "Busy," he said.

Instead of leaving, Habib walked over and pressed the clicker on the telephone, cutting off the line. "I'm not in touch with you anymore."

"Don't say that," said Raj, irritated at the high-handed way Habib had shut off the call.

"I'm going to be blunt," said Habib. "No one has been in touch with you. We're supposed to travel in packs. That's part of the training." Habib frowned. "Don't tell me you've been busy either. This is psychiatry, my friend, remember?"

"Yes."

"Then give me one lunch, and we can discuss your state of mind, which may be morbidly cheerful," said Habib. "Although I doubt it."

"Nothing's wrong with me," said Raj.

"In your circumstances, I would say you might be wrong on that score," said Habib.

"Is that what you think, that I'm disturbed and hiding it? Why would I do that?" Raj asked, controlling his temper.

Habib said, "You're not in the normal world, in case you haven't noticed yet. This is shrink town. Forget privacy or the dignity of grief. We account for all our feelings to each other. We rip them to shreds and out of those shreds we find out how our patients tick, because we've seen the tiniest hint of ourselves. You don't get to opt out."

"Did someone send you around? Is that it?" asked Raj.

"No one had to. Your behavior sent me around," said Habib. "Look at yourself. You're so high I wonder what you're telling your patients. You're going to be cut, man, if you keep on this way." Raj let him talk. With every word the distance between them widened, and that was all right. He needed only one friend from now on.

"I'm not here to spoil your trip," Habib was saying. "But I looked over your charts recently. You're too directive. You're giving cues to these people, and then they're trotting out what they know you want to hear."

"There's nothing wrong with my charts. Show me where," Raj said, starting to get hot.

"Christ!" Habib shook his head and left without answering. Raj sat in his chair letting the shock waves recede. He still cradled the telephone receiver in his hand. He waited for signs of self-doubt, and when they didn't come, he dialed again. Maya answered after three rings.

"I found Sasha," Raj said.

"At the bar last night? And?" Maya sounded relieved but guarded.

"And she's found someone to stay with, a home away from home, I think. She looked okay. She seems to be keeping up with her meds."

"Thank God." A warm wave of feeling came across the line. "When's she coming back?"

"We didn't talk about that yet. I just wanted to observe her," Raj lied. He would try to keep Serena and his own doings out of the picture.

"May I make an observation?" Maya asked.

"Go ahead."

"You were ready to snatch her out of purgatory when I left, and now you've decided to observe her?"

"Once I saw that she was okay, I felt it would be a mistake to disturb her. I walked in suddenly. She might have gone off. It's tricky."

Raj waited. It sounded plausible to him. Maya came back softer. "The important thing is that she didn't fall over the edge. We didn't lose her," she said.

"Right. Exactly."

"Then shall we celebrate? That's not the right word, but you know what I mean," said Maya, hesitating. "If you feel up to it."

"Okay, sure," said Raj, not at all sure.

They agreed to meet on Saturday evening. Just before leaving his shift, Clarence found Raj near the vending machines.

"Hey," Clarence said, searching for quarters in his white coat.

"You part of the posse?" Raj asked.

"That depends," said Clarence, who wasn't usually

evasive. "Some people think you're getting a bit extreme."

"Is this a way of saying that I want my patients to get better too fast? Sometimes I think no one around here believes in breakthroughs," Raj said.

"A breakthrough isn't something you force."

"Meaning what?"

"Meaning that every patient in this place has one thing in mind, and it's not getting better. It's escape. Getting better is hard work, escape is easy. And it feels good. What is your opinion about escape?" asked Clarence.

Raj hesitated. Clarence wasn't trying to nail him, he just wanted assurance that Raj himself wasn't escaping. In therapy escape is a primary danger of the trade. It means thinking you are personally anointed to heal your patient; it means giving in to the fantasy that you are all-knowing and all-powerful. Above all, it means that only you and no one else can find the magic words that will bring healing to someone's troubled mind.

"I'm not forcing anybody," Raj said, making sure to keep his tone within respectful bounds. "Maybe I'm being a little more intimate than some people around here choose to be. We don't have to be distant demigods. I like getting closer to my patients."

Clarence listened with his eyes closely held on Raj. "You've got no business being intimate with anybody right now," he said abruptly.

"I didn't mean it that way."

"Not overtly, but there's more than one way to seduce. Therapy isn't about getting your needs fulfilled. I'm on your side, and I don't tell tales. But we both know this isn't the most stable period of your life." Clarence's voice lost its edge and he put a hand on Raj's shoulder. "Be careful with your judgment, that's all. I can guarantee you that it's off. Now, let me treat you to some lousy coffee." Clarence dropped some coins into the machine and held up his fist, prepared to pound the thing if they didn't drop in.

WHEN HE FINALLY got back to his apartment, Raj fell into a deep sleep. Ten hours later he woke up, and his elation was gone. A sober gray light filtered through the blinds. After his shave he found a message on his machine that he must have slept through. It was from Serena. "Love, are you there? . . . Okay, here goes anyway. I told our friend she should go back to school and get adjusted again. It was time. She probably won't call you, but if she does, I think you should know that someone at school is the baby's father. Name of Barry,

I believe it is. She says she didn't sleep with anyone else when she was out on the street, but that might be iffy. She doesn't know what state she was in all the time."

The machine clicked off at the end of the tape before Serena said anything more, and she hadn't called back. Raj realized that he didn't have her phone number, but the news was dramatic enough. He thought about it as he dressed and prepared to go downtown to meet Maya. They had agreed to meet at one of the Indian cafés on Fifty-sixth Street, the way they had before Raj left.

When Raj stepped inside the restaurant, he saw a Ganesh statue draped with colored lights, its elephant trunk twinkling red and green. He had blocked out the holiday season completely up until then. Maya stood up and waved from a corner table. She seemed at ease throughout the meal. She never mentioned Molly or touched upon Raj's loss, waiting to take the lead from him. But she was very concerned when Raj brought up Sasha and the likelihood that they would have to confront Barry again.

"I thought you were too rough on him before," Maya said, "but I guess not."

"Barry's not going to stand by her. Our best hope is that he caves right away and accepts that the baby is his, especially if he's telling the truth about only sleeping

with her once," said Raj. He could already foresee battles, perhaps court intervention. The girl's history of
psychosis would work against her, and if her distraught
parents went to court to get a DNA sample from Barry
to prove that he was the father, any half-competent
defense attorney would tear Sasha's story apart. There
was no way for Raj to piece together a reliable version
of Sasha's sexual life.

They left the restaurant, but it was not yet ten, and
Maya wanted to see the tree in Rockefeller Center. Raj
had drunk a glass of wine on an empty stomach, and
when she slipped her hand into his, he left it there. The
walk down Fifth Avenue with its festoons of white
lights filled his senses. The vibrant city was asking him
a silent question: What makes you believe there is
another reality? Raj knew the adage about the many
who are called and the few who are chosen. Why were
the chosen supposed to be the lucky ones? Clarence's
warning about his impaired judgment hinted at the
troubles Raj might be tumbling into.

When he leaned over the railing and saw the skaters
at the sunken rink on the plaza, their whirling bodies
made Raj pensive.

"What are you thinking?" Maya asked.

"I was thinking about the soul. How it might travel
in circles, just like them." He pointed to the skaters

below. "I keep feeling that the same patterns are repeating themselves over and over. Every day I do something different, say different words, worry over different thoughts. But what if my soul is circling me, always coming back to something it wants me to know?"

"That's the first Indian thing I've ever heard you say," Maya remarked.

It was true. Souls don't travel in straight lines in India. Although Raj had never returned to India, the old childhood lessons started up again. He remembered that souls aren't arrows shot by a person's actions to heaven or hell, where they will stay forever. Instead the soul is like a circling bird floating above the shifting adventures of a lifetime. There is never eternal damnation or eternal reward. When one lifetime is over and the sum of good and bad is added up, the soul changes its path ever so slightly. Dipping or rising, it will return again to the lessons of life.

Such a belief provides for second chances. No action is so unique that it doesn't get repeated many times, until every bit of savor has been drained. Is this greed or simply thoroughness? Perhaps it is true that deep inside, our being knows the truth. We have lived too long to believe in final results. Like skaters colliding and crossing on silvery ice, holding hands for a swift round and then parting again, souls fly together and asunder. No

one is new to anyone else. No one is a stranger to anyone else. The dance is eternal, and our only choice is
how long to spend with the partners who fascinate us.

"I've had enough. It's getting cold," Raj said, harden-
ing himself against the disappointment he saw in Maya's
face. It was no good giving her hope when he still had
promises to keep. He turned away from the railing with
a slight sense of vertigo, so he didn't trust the sight of
Molly coming toward him. She was in a black wool coat
with a fox collar—he recognized it immediately as one
of the few things of her mother's that Molly wore.

Why now? Raj thought.

"Because of her." Molly was looking at Maya, who
was stamping her feet against the cold, waiting on Raj.

What about her?

"You belong together. She represents happiness and a
future," Molly said.

That's not true. You're my happiness.

"I told you I made a bargain. It brought me here, but
whatever you learn from me, Maya is the one you'll live
it with."

Raj shook his head, deeply distressed. *We're together
because we promised to be, forever.*

"That won't change. Just be patient and see," said
Molly.

Raj ran toward her as if Maya didn't exist. He felt her tug at his sleeve.

"Don't run away," Maya said. "Why do you look like that?"

"Let go of me. I don't need you," Raj snapped, resisting Maya's pull.

"Maybe you need someone to remind you what's real. I'm not blind. She's what you think about. You keep seeing her, and that isn't the way to get better." Although a gentle person, Maya stood her ground, saying her words without blame.

Raj realized that his chest was heaving. "Who are you to say what's real?" he shot back. "I know what I want."

"All right," Maya said. "Have the impossible if you want it, but you'll have to get over it. I can wish that for you, at least."

It was the most powerful thing she had said since their breakup. Raj's brain was stormed with confusion. Maya seemed to be taking the steps toward him that Molly foresaw.

"I know you think you're right," he mumbled, which said nothing.

"So you did see something just now? It's all right," Maya said. When he didn't respond she went on. "I'm not here to deny you someone you loved. How could

I? Molly was never real to me, so we aren't enemies. You understand that, don't you?"

Raj stared at Maya as if she were a talking puppet. Finally he said, "What's unreal for you is too real for me."

Whether to calm him down or keep him beside her, Maya found an unexpected angle. "After I was born, we stayed in India long enough for me to remember my ayah. She was the oldest nursemaid any of the families around us hired, a fierce old thing. I think she had tended my mother and maybe her mother, who knows? Ayah was very superstitious, and when she had any problems she went to the temple for answers. My mother couldn't disapprove, so if my nurse had a niece who was stricken with typhoid or a neighbor whose husband was beating her, she dragged me off with her.

"Only she was lying. We didn't go to temple but to a graveyard. I had never even imagined such a place, since Hindus aren't buried in cemeteries. Ayah would sit me down on the pavement inside the gates and draw a circle of chalk around me, with dire warnings that if I stepped out of the circle, horrible demons would eat me alive. I was scared to death and spent half the time crying while she was gone. The woman always came back with a determined look on her face. She had her answer.

"One day I was big enough so that curiosity overcame fear. When my ayah left, I broke out of the circle and followed her. It was a very decrepit cemetery, even for India, the ground littered with things you didn't want to look down and see. I lost track of her for a minute, then there she was on her knees, talking to herself in the rubble of gravestones. I crept up and touched her shoulder. She screamed. For a split second I saw them, the ones she got her answers from. Ayah's yell made me jump, but once she got through scolding me and yanking my hair, she was sure that I had seen them, too. I think it pleased her. She treated me much better after that. We made a pact not to tell my parents, and I never did."

"I thought you were rooting for reality," said Raj. "Your goal is to get me to come back to it from wherever you think I've gone."

"Yes," said Maya, "but the circle might be wider than you give me credit for. And I might be brave enough to walk outside it."

"Ah."

10.

Raj couldn't sleep after leaving Maya at the subway station. He lay awake staring at the ceiling. It took hours to recover from the shock of seeing Molly and Maya together at the same time. Unless he counted the night he had taken Maya to the theater, Raj had been able to keep them apart. Doing so had eased his conscience, but it hadn't erased the truth. He loved them both, and both were still equally alive.

A sane person would have said that Raj's predicament

was impossible. A man can't love two women when one is a ghost. Yet in some ways Maya was a ghost, too. Even if Raj could pull her back, the past couldn't be revived. If he gave himself totally to Molly, however, she couldn't be his.

The slatted blinds threw bars of cold winter moonlight across the bed. Raj's mind kept racing to find a solution. Molly alone held the key, but he couldn't find her. How many hours had passed? Six, eight? She didn't appear again. When Raj reached inside to hear her voice, he heard only the whir of his own thoughts. There was no presence in the darkness except the cold moonlight that had crept up to cover his face.

At four A.M. he finally jumped out of bed, certain that only one person could understand. He stood stamping in the freezing wind until the first bus came. An hour later, when Raj was walking through thick frost to the door of Serena's bungalow, the sun was still an hour from rising. He squatted on the steps to conserve body heat and waited. He wouldn't knock until there were signs of life inside. By the time Serena opened the door in her old wrapper, Raj was all but frozen. She pulled him into the kitchen.

"If you're going to die for love, you might as well do it with some food inside you," she said.

"Just coffee." The sight of her revived Raj's spirits.

They sat together around the cheap pine dinette table rather than at the breakfast bar.

"I saw her," Raj began. "More than once. She speaks to me."

"What does she say?" Serena asked.

"She's teaching me. Mostly when I'm with patients. She's leading me toward something."

"Healing," said Serena calmly, "if you're lucky."

"What do you mean?" asked Raj.

"Ghosts don't lead to healing, but if she isn't a ghost, then something very important and right could be happening."

Raj desperately wanted to believe her, but he faltered. "It's getting more complicated. Maya—she was my fiancée—is beginning to suspect. I can't come out and tell her, but if I don't—" His voice trailed off.

"Let her suspect," said Serena. "This is a breakthrough."

"To what? I'm totally turned around. It seems I'm only real when Molly's inside me, and who would believe that?"

"Anyone who has ever loved deeply," said Serena firmly. "Millions of people long to find someone who is dead and speak with them again. To you it happened. So you must pay attention and find out why." Raj kept quiet.

"I see," said Serena. "You haven't lost your obsessive streak. You want more encounters. You want to see her again and again."

"Yes, absolutely." Raj felt no hesitation; the alternative was an empty hole where once Molly had been.

Serena said, "Do you want to move in with her? What if she uses your toothbrush or starts flirting with other dead guys?"

"You think I'm fooling myself," Raj said.

"I'm not taking anything away from you," Serena replied. "You're allowed to get what you want." If she hadn't added that, Raj might have bolted from the table and left. As it was, he seized the snippet being held out to him.

"This is what I want," he said fervently, "even if I wind up completely miserable. Even if I have to give up everything."

"Why are you so reckless?" Serena said sharply. "All this crying and being in love with darkness. All this self-pity. It's not how these things are done."

"How are they done?" asked Raj, calming his emotion even though it was like a truck rolling downhill.

"Molly knows," said Serena, "assuming that you're lucky and she is what you believe her to be."

She got up and pulled her wrapper tighter. "It takes

a while for the house to warm up. Can you turn off the coffee and make yourself something while I dress?"

Raj nodded and went into the kitchen, but he found it impossible to eat—a few minutes later he was standing down the hallway outside Serena's bedroom door. It was quiet except for an occasional rustling from the other side. He heard shoes dropping to the floor in the bedroom. She must have sat down to put on makeup. A whiff of perfume slid under the door. Raj remembered Molly's words about Maya.

You belong together. Whatever you learn from me, Maya is the one you'll live it with.

So Molly had told him what the solution was, only he couldn't decipher what it meant. Raj wandered back to the living room and sank into the same worn armchair that Sasha had been sitting in. When Serena appeared again, she sat on the sofa opposite and considered him.

"You said that Molly speaks to you about your patients. Is she right?" Serena asked.

"Yes. From their reactions, I'd say she's amazingly right," said Raj.

"How do you explain that?"

"I can't. It mystifies me even while I'm doing what she wants and saying what she tells me," said Raj.

"That's good," Serena remarked. Before Raj could

protest, she raised her hand. "When I was a little girl, there was an old woman named Amelia Sanchez with two broken legs from a fishing-boat accident. Amelia had been confined to her house for many years, and she grew quite withered from sitting in the sun beside her crutches waiting for the world to bring her something good. Her husband had drowned in that same accident, so she had little more than scraps to eat, which were brought around by her children when they remembered.

"You are a sophisticated person, so you have no interest in contacting ghosts. Instead you want the impossible. But in my village people were happy with ghosts. Lonely Amelia became a sort of wonder-worker, and whoever needed to talk to a dead relative came to her, even if the priest was watching. Except for my mother, who scoffed and said that no one could be that gullible. 'I've seen that old cripple wheedle information, until by now she knows everything about everybody,' my mother would say. 'She stores up all the gossip and then feeds it back from the dead. Ridiculous.'

"What no one knew was that I saw the ghosts myself, so I could tell that Amelia wasn't faking. Not that she was above throwing in a juicy scrap or two, just to make sure her audience returned. In truth ghosts are very unhappy. They refuse to accept the kindness of death.

They, too, are afflicted with expectations. They expect to come back or to say something important they forgot to say before. Some simply want revenge. Above all, they cling to this world because they are afraid to go into the unknown.

"I kept my secret for a long time, going around with plantain fritters and dried coconut flakes so that I could sit near the old *bruja* and hear what she told people. Then I went to my mother and said, 'You're wrong, Amelia really talks to ghosts, but you are also right. It is just gossip, only gossip from the other world, which doesn't make it any better.' I didn't go back after that."

"You were a very strong-willed child," said Raj.

Serena grinned. "Things don't change much. I decided then and there never to be lonely like Amelia Sanchez and never to wait by the door for the world to bring me answers. I decided not to cling to the past. I got rid of expectations; I gave up foolish hopes; I lost my fear of the unknown. But none of that is extraordinary."

"Yes, it is. You're selling yourself short," said Raj.

"No, the extraordinary thing was about death. I looked without being afraid and saw that death is not an ending. Death is where disappointment stops, and something wonderful opens up—the complete unknown. If I could, I would stand up before the millions and shout, *Don't be afraid. Death is a leap of the soul.* But the people who would understand probably wouldn't be in the audience." She said this last without irony or regret. To her it was just a fact to be accepted.

As he listened, an image came to Raj's mind. He saw people milling around in the dark, each with a flashlight. They were in an art gallery, and as they went from picture to picture, the flashlight narrowed their vision so that they saw only one image at a time. What they missed was the entire room, which was papered with masterpieces.

And then Raj had an insight. *Life is the art gallery. I only have a flashlight, but Molly can see the whole room.* That was the leap her soul had taken.

"I can answer your question," Raj said. "About how Molly knows about my patients. She sees them all at once, every part of them. Death has given her wide-angle vision."

Serena nodded. "Which is why I'm sure she isn't a ghost. You gave me the clue. Now you have to take the next step and start seeing her as something different from the woman who loves you."

"What?" asked Raj, feeling a pang of anxiety.

"You'll have to start seeing her as a soul," Serena said.

Raj got to his feet, noticing that the yellow morning sun was now level with his eyes. He must have been there for two hours. "You're asking me for a kind of surrender," he said. "You're asking me to give her up when everything in me screams to possess her. I can't make promises. To me she's still the woman I can't live without. But at least I'm not seeing ghosts. On that we agree."

Serena laughed loudly, and Raj could feel the tips of his ears burning. "The problem, doll, isn't about seeing ghosts," she said. "In your case, it's about not making love to them."

At ten o'clock, when Raj stepped off the elevator onto the pavilion, there was blood on the walls. A huge red smear began chest high and dripped to the floor not ten feet from the nurses' station.

"Claudia," a voice said. It was Mona, who for some reason didn't look horrified. "She's been throwing cans again, only this time she opens them first. Nice. That's tomato soup. Come with me."

Raj followed her to Claudia's room. She was tied to her bed with restraints, and his entrance was signaled by a horrifying shriek. Claudia's head whipped from side to side. She was trying to avoid the rubber mouth gag being suspended over her face by Mathers.

"No one has hurt you and no one is going to," Mathers said in a measured voice. "You had a seizure, do you understand?" He looked over his shoulder as Raj approached.

"Bastard! Criminal!" Claudia shrieked.

"I wasn't going to put it back in," Mathers said, "unless we needed to protect you from yourself."

"You're not going to put it back in, no matter what," said Raj angrily. "I'm here, Claudia. It's going to be all right." On the other side of the bed an orderly and nurse stood guard. Everyone was tensely focused on their charge.

"Bastard!" Claudia kept screaming, ignoring Raj.

"Dr. Mathers, will you step away?" said Raj, giving him a look that stopped any protest. Mathers bowed out silently, taking the orderly and nurse with him. Raj didn't care at that moment about the medical situation. He was too shocked by the change in Claudia's appearance. Her eyes were bulging and rolling in two directions like a mad horse. Chunks of hair were gone, exposing livid patches of scalp. She looked twenty years older.

"I'm here now," Raj repeated. He gave Claudia a minute to recognize him, and when she did, her eyes holding on to him, he released one of the bands around her wrist. Gnarled knots stood out on her forearm, as if preparing to take a wild swing, but the muscles relaxed. He took off the other restraint and sat down.

"Is the light too bright?" he asked, to gauge how in touch she was. Claudia scowled and shook her head. Raj turned the switch down anyway. "Wow," he said.

That was the extent of their conversation for the next five minutes. Claudia clenched her teeth and stared stubbornly at the ceiling.

"Like fucking hell I had a seizure," she finally said in a voice close to a yell. "You were supposed to be here!"

"I wish I had been."

His placating tone stopped her rage in mid-torrent, and another five minutes of silence ensued. Then Claudia said, "I got back here fast this time."

"Record time," Raj remarked, making sure to show not the slightest sign of argument. "I thought you had a long weekend, or was it supposed to be a week this time? Something happened."

"You could say." Claudia ran her hand up into her scalp to smooth her hair out, only to feel one of the bald patches. "Christ!" she muttered bitterly.

"Do you remember what happened to you, exactly?" Raj asked.

"Fucking Stanley Klemper happened to me, about twenty-six years ago," she spat out. "But this is the worst. I can't hide this." Some recollection yet to be revealed came to mind, and her voice faltered. Now she whispered with deep, almost uncontrollable sadness. "The worst *ever*."

"What were you fighting about?" Raj asked.

"You," said Claudia.

"What about me?" Raj tried not to look startled.

"He hates that you're trying to change me. He says that shrinks just meddle in other people's business and ruin their lives. I tried to stand up to him, and he went berserk."

"Violence can be very intimidating," Raj said, "but even if Stanley hates it, do you want to change?"

Claudia nodded. Though frightened and upset, her eyes were trusting. Raj believed—or wanted to believe—that this episode was not backsliding. "If Stanley is making me an issue," he said, "it's because he's threatened. He has all kinds of images of you. One image is the woman he married; another is the woman he can cheat on and get away with it; another is the woman he wants to love but can't find a way to. He feels guilty, and lashing out at you may be the only way he can deal with that."

This won't work.

What? Raj thought.

This won't work.

His heart skipped a beat. Molly. There was no mistaking her voice inside him. Raj's reaction was so strong, such a mixture of elation, relief, and gratitude that he lost his focus on Claudia. She had been listening carefully, and as Raj's words sank in, she visibly calmed.

"Stanley says if I keep seeing you, no good will come of it," Claudia said with emotion. "I know I can't keep relying on you—" Her voice trailed off, and there was again a long silence.

"You can always rely on me," Raj said, but his mind went elsewhere.

Listen to me, said Molly's voice, and Raj could hear laughter in it. *This won't work because there is no Stanley!*

He was speechless, staring hard at Claudia, who took no notice. Her fingers wandered to a bare patch on her skull, then quickly drew away.

"I need to get better," she mumbled, on the verge of sleep. Raj left quickly. He could still hear Molly's laughter, but everything else was in turmoil. Anger and humiliation coursed through his body as he rushed down the hall.

"Dr. Rabban?" a man's voice said.

Raj saw Claudia in his mind's eye, and she seemed veiled. The face and body were hers, the words coming out of her mouth fit what he wanted to hear. But she had been playing him in order to keep a secret. Why?

"I need to speak to you if you don't mind."

The voice intruded again. Raj saw Halverson in front of him, putting a hand on his shoulder. "Do you have a moment?" Halverson said.

"Yes, I'm sorry, I was distracted."

Raj could tell that Halverson wanted to walk with him down the corridor, so they did. For the first minute, all Raj could think about was getting away so he could ask Molly everything about the deception she had just revealed.

"So do you think that was wise?" Halverson asked.

"What?"

"Getting close to Mrs. Klemper. It's not the right technique, and I've been worried." Halverson's voice sounded concerned rather than threatening. The talk about Raj's impaired judgment was spreading. That must be it.

"I think I understand her," Raj said cautiously.

"Then how do you explain her sudden explosive episode?" asked Halverson.

"There was a violent fight at home, and she—" Raj stopped short, suddenly realizing that anything he said about Claudia could be totally false. "I need to ask her more questions," he said.

"Why would you believe her answers? She's too invested in you. Instead of seeing that and stopping it, you seem to have encouraged it. Some might say you are responsible for what is happening now."

They were still walking together down the hall, but out of the corner of his eye Raj saw that Halverson was more than concerned. He was controlled, but furious.

"In order to keep patients from giving in to fantasy," he said with mounting accusation, "the therapist must know the difference between fantasy and reality. Yet you don't even know if this woman is delusional. Either she has sucked you into her fantasy world or you have sucked her into yours. If it's the first, we can chalk it up to naïveté and inexperience. There's nothing wrong with being raw. But if it's the second, that's downright criminal in my view."

Raj was aware that people were staring. As rare as it was for Halverson to lose his temper, it was practically unthinkable that he would do it outside the office.

"I still don't know what this is about," Raj said quietly.

"Don't you?" Halverson was holding up a chart and waving it under his nose. "Did you even bother to interview this woman and get the basic facts?"

"Yes, of course."

"Really?" Halverson opened the chart to the first page. His long finger pointed to one line near the bottom. "Do you see that, Doctor?" Halverson asked. *"There is no Stanley!"*

Fury showed in Halverson's voice now. "Her husband was confined to a wheelchair for the past five years with MS and died on April tenth of last year."

Raj could have said, "I know." He could have taken the blame for screwing up and for letting his inexperience get the better of him. But he knew this was a turning point. Screwing up only mattered if he accepted Halverson's way, but he didn't, not anymore. Molly's voice had quit laughing inside. She was simply watching him now, with a gaze of love.

Raj's silence caught Halverson off guard. He drew back. "We all screw up," Halverson said, "but you were taken in, and that happens only when a therapist wants to be taken in. Don't you agree?" Raj nodded; he could see that Halverson was running out of steam.

"It is my guess that you overlooked this patient's obvious ploys, her blatant attempts to win your approval. Why would you do that?"

"I'm not sure. But I am sure of what's real. You're wrong about that," Raj said.

"What makes you think that, young man?" snapped Halverson. His powers of insight were being challenged.

"Because I know Stanley is irrelevant," Raj said. "When we get to the bottom of it, Claudia's going to be cured, with or without him."

Halverson was incredulous. "You can stand here and say that? Perhaps you work miracles undercover," he said, "perhaps the suffering of others causes you too much pain, perhaps you simply want to be loved and don't know the right place to look. Does any of this put a damper on your certainty?"

"No, I don't think so," Raj said with firmness.

Halverson glared at him. "You have a patient who has inflicted some sort of wound to herself, even though it looks like no more than a black eye and pulled hair, fortunately for you. It's also likely that your treatment has made her problems worse rather than better. Consider these issues and then we'll talk."

Halverson turned his back, and Raj tried to avoid the eyes that had been devouring his humiliation. Most were patients, since staff members had the decency to walk past with bowed heads. Raj kept walking toward his original destination, the residents' office.

"Crash and burn time, huh?" Habib was sympathetic as Raj walked in the office. The gist of what had happened, if not every gory detail, would already be flying around the pavilion.

"It's not like they weren't gunning for me," Raj said.

"You're an idealist, that's the bottom line," said Habib, "and weird as it sounds, this isn't much of a job for idealists."

"What's the alternative?" Raj knew the answer—Molly's answer—but he wanted to hear from Habib before he walked out on this part of his life.

Habib shook his head. "For you there might not be one. You forgot how mean patients in this place can be. Crazy is a mean place. You idealists don't like to admit that."

Habib said all this with a bit of caution, which was unlike him, as if he feared ripping apart a fragile creature. But Raj wasn't feeling torn up.

Time to go, said Molly's voice.

"I'm going home," said Raj. "I don't think anyone will miss me the rest of the day." He suppressed a smile at seeing Habib's long face.

This person is afraid for you. Reassure him with the truth.

"I'm not in trouble," Raj said, looking Habib in the eye. "If I hadn't gotten close to Claudia, she wouldn't have improved. Even if she fooled me with her fantasies, she did it because I gave her a taste of something—call it by its right name—love. She wanted more love, so she painted herself as the victim. Her methods were bizarre, and predictably they came back to hurt her, but it isn't evil or twisted or crazy to want love."

"I see," said Habib. "Well." If Raj expected him to choke up with admiration, it wasn't happening. "I'm looking at your face," Habib said, "and you still think you're right."

"Yeah."

Don't fight him. He got it, said Molly's voice.

All at once, Habib was far from Raj's mind. Knowing where he had to be, Raj turned and left without another word. Claudia was sitting up in bed with her lunch tray, contemplating a bowl of cubed red Jell-O.

"You're back," she said neutrally, not giving away how much she already knew of the incident in the corridor. Raj sat on the edge of the bed. His closeness made Claudia flinch slightly.

"This isn't a session," he said. "We can just talk."

Claudia hung her head and put the lunch tray back on its rolling stand. "I had you going for a while," she said without much conviction.

"That you did."

Don't wait for her story. Tell her.

Raj said, "I think you turned Stanley into a monster because you loved him too much. By telling me how abusive he was, you protected feelings that might dissolve and wash away. Something like that?"

Claudia was looking away. She gripped her hands to keep from pushing Raj away.

"You were desperate to protect those precious feelings. They were all you had. People don't feel desperate from ordinary love. I imagine Stanley was far from ordinary in your eyes," said Raj softly.

It took a moment before Claudia could speak. "In his day, he was the most wonderful man I could have dreamed of," she said in a faraway voice. "Did you know my doctor, the one from before?" she asked. Raj shook his head. "He liked dreams and other stupid stuff. Whether I loved my mother. It made no sense, and every day I was watching my Stanley getting worse and worse. I never felt I deserved him. His parents said he was a fool to marry me. It took a long time to turn that man into a vegetable, but eventually it was diaper changes and feeding liquids through a tube."

"You felt a lot of panic," said Raj. "More than you could handle."

"My world fell apart, and it wasn't much of a world to begin with." Claudia laughed with faint bitterness. "I guess you'd say I wasn't put together very well, not for a long time."

She talked simply, without trying to win Raj over, and then she stopped. Her face wore the blank look of someone whom life has outwitted many times. Raj regarded Claudia's gray face and for a moment saw someone else.

In the early days when he and Habib were buddies, they had gone out on a double date. Habib's girl, whose name was Christie, clung to him like an infant and kept her head on his shoulder while everyone else read the menu. She laughed uncontrollably at anything anybody said, her mouth gaping open in mid-chew so that you could see the food. Raj was shocked to find out that Habib had picked her up that afternoon at the outpatient clinic.

"It's not like she's a patient," Habib said in his own defense. "She brought in her manic father, who was running up all his credit cards. He tried to charge a new Volvo." Raj didn't look too convinced, and Habib grinned. "So she's a little loosely sutured. I don't mind. Let it be her mystery."

"She has about as much mystery as a ruptured spleen. You can't do this," Raj said.

"I'm just letting nature take its course. What's so bad in that?" said Habib. He dumped the girl two weeks later, once they'd had sex.

Claudia was that girl thirty years later. She was a naked soul wrapped in too much experience, so that underneath the thick wool of her past, her soul couldn't be seen anymore, either by her or anyone else. Raj had to take it on faith that despite everything, a soul wants to be seen. That is its only desire in the world, and the hardest to win.

I want to lift away her pain, thought Raj. He waited for Molly's answer.

Not yet. There's more to learn. But soon.

"I have to go talk to my supervisor," Raj said, getting up from Claudia's bed.

"Will they fire you?" she asked.

"The worst would be just to let me slide out after the year is up. Don't worry." Raj smiled and headed for the door.

"I'm sorry," Claudia said to his retreating back.

Soon, repeated Molly's voice inside.

11.

WHEN RAJ WALKED into Halverson's office to be grilled, Halverson had him sit in the sagging leather arm-chair reserved for his private patients. He expressed his own personal disappointment that a promising young resident would lose his way.

"Reality is an elephant that we can't move. None of us," said Halverson. "It just stands there; it is what it is. Mental patients don't believe in that fact. Somewhere along the line they become very angry that reality doesn't budge because they want it to. It doesn't hand them love when they most need it. It doesn't go out of its way to console them or protect them from being hurt. Reality isn't Mommy."

Raj felt a small jolt. He was sure for a second that Halverson had said, "Reality isn't Molly."

Halverson went on, "When someone is angry enough at reality, they start pretending it's not there. They run off into the forest of fantasy, and under the trees they nurse all their secret wounds. Their disappointment is deep and tragic, and to be all alone is frightening, but people become acclimated. There's no other way."

Halverson paused to poke a steel tobacco tamper around in the bowl of his pipe. With his grizzled beard, he looked amazingly like a sad old ape.

Raj could have resigned then and there. Only he wanted to laugh. He particularly wanted to laugh at Halverson's elephant. It was such a fraud. A crock. An excuse you could hold up so that you never, ever looked behind the curtain.

"What if I could show you that you're wrong," said Raj when Halverson was done.

"And how do you intend to do that?" Halverson replied impatiently.

"By cutting through. By making reality change for these patients," said Raj.

Halverson shook his head. "I don't think you've grasped what I was saying."

"To me, you've been saying that loving these people is feeble and pointless. Insanity is too powerful, and reality doesn't give a shit. Is that about right?" asked Raj.

Halverson's benevolent calm had vanished. "I could easily accuse you of hubris," he said. "Do you think you know more than all the therapists in this hospital?"

Without asking if he could leave, Raj got up and walked out. He had no ground to stand on, nothing that Halverson would accept. But he didn't intend to crash and burn, either. Snow had fallen in the city, enough to give a soft squishing sound to the traffic. Crosswalks were rapidly turning into moats of brown slush. Raj took the stairs up to his apartment and found two messages on the machine. One was from his parents reminding him about the Christmas holidays. The other was from Maya.

"Barry came to talk to me today. He's freaked out about the baby—surprise—and he says it's not his. I told him we should discuss this in front of Sasha. Not the news he wanted to hear. I went down to see if she was home, but she wasn't, and by the time I got back, Barry had run away. What do I do now? Please call."

When Raj called her back, Maya noticed something in his voice. "You sound up," she said.

"I've made some decisions," said Raj.

"About what?"

"Several things. But there's one particular one. You mentioned something about raising the dead. I realized that Molly isn't dead, not for me."

Maya paused to take this in. "I'm glad," she said.

"You may not understand this, but that decision makes me want to see you again. The way we used to," said Raj.

"Why?" Maya didn't sound shocked; she was patiently piecing together what Raj intended.

"Because there's not a choice anymore. It's not you or Molly," Raj said.

"You want us both?" said Maya.

"I always have," said Raj. "I just didn't know how, and now I do. If you thought I ever stopped loving you, it's my fault. I never did. You told me you could live in a bigger circle or maybe even step outside. Well, I'm asking you to."

"You're asking me to include a dead woman in our relationship? I don't mean to put it that way, but it's the truth, isn't it?" said Maya. "How would that work?"

"It would work if neither of us judges the other. It would work if we don't try to possesses the other," said Raj. He realized that if Serena had asked him to surrender, now he was asking Maya.

Maya said, "This is very strange. We have to talk about it in person."

"Agreed."

Raj would come to Maya's apartment as soon as he could get ready. But she didn't want him to stop there. "We have to follow Sasha's trail," she said. "Let's see if she's at home first. Then we'll get to us."

"Let's say an hour?" asked Raj.

"Fine." There was a pause. "If you thought I ever stopped loving you, it's my fault, too," said Maya. As she hung up, the last thing Raj heard in her voice was a struggle among relief, confusion, and hope. She needed more time and perhaps more space than he had taken into account.

Raj stood under a hot shower in his moldy bathroom feeling strong. The confidence he'd found in facing up to Halverson was turning into ebullience. He was going to have Molly because *It* would give her to him. Serena had told him so, but Raj wasn't just relying on that. He knew. Before his mind could reason things through, a core of belief had already formed inside him. Claudia had taught him something immense.

The soul wants to be seen.

Most people are humiliated by this need. It's too innocent in a world where innocence, as a survival skill, counts for nothing. To show your soul undressed in public is indecent exposure. Other people will turn away from you, as they always have from madmen, saints, poets, visionaries, and geniuses. But a motley crew of the crazy and inspired share a secret. Once you get past the shock of being naked, something incredible appears: *It.*

It was the force that threw Molly into his life. *It* was the seed that she wanted to sprout. When people awaken, the light that dawns is *It.* And *It* would untangle all the conflict that Raj had wrapped around himself.

Now Raj knew why Serena had told him he needed to see Molly as a soul, not as a dead woman he once had loved in life. When you see anyone as a soul, all they are is *It.* Body and personality melt away, leaving only the mystery. When you see with the eyes of the soul, there is no difference between the living and the dead. All are naked together.

Raj stayed too long under the hot water and came out sweating and faintly nauseous. Wrapping a towel around his waist, he opened the bathroom window and stood there, letting cold air and flicking snowflakes waft around his body. Then he got dressed and immediately headed out. He hailed a cab going downtown.

"Take Broadway," he told the driver.

"You'll lose ten minutes in Times Square. We should take the West Side Highway," the driver advised.

"I don't care," said Raj. Like many other things he had been avoiding, he never walked down Broadway anymore. It had reminded him too painfully of summer nights with Molly, but a hunter follows his pain.

Despite the snow, the crowds were thick and on the move. Every crosswalk was jammed through the red lights, leaving the taxis to crawl or come to a dead halt as dozens of bodies swept around them. The eight-story televison screen that wrapped around the corner of the NASDAQ building lit up the night like a Technicolor bonfire. Huge billboards rose to the sky with gaudy glee.

"Let me out here," Raj called, tapping on the plastic shield.

"We ain't anywhere," said the driver, who was getting annoyed. Raj tossed him some bills and dove into the crowd. It was exhilarating. People were packed so tight that he could see steam rising from their bodies. The mob moved en masse. Raj circled the block where the Disney empire had moved in and taken over. There were no more porno shops or strip clubs to be seen. Mouse conquers sleaze.

Ten feet away two black kids with a boom box were

break-dancing on the sidewalk. They twirled and kicked on their backs, ignoring the dirty slush around them. One could spin standing on his head, drawing hoots and applause from the spectators. Raj felt incredibly free, but he had to move on. He was a hunter.

He knew he was in a strange state. The faces around him were mostly black and Latino, with the occasional dotting of a stray white person, yet each could be read like a journal. They weren't the faces of the faceless. He saw fear walk by and boredom, he saw anger bottled up, and even some love. If he could have talked with any of these wanderers for five minutes, he swore he would have known them down to their shoes.

Raj had misjudged the cold, and his thin leather jacket let the wind cut right through him. But he didn't want to duck into the warm, greasy-smelling eateries that opened onto the street. He rounded the block onto Eighth Avenue with the intention of circling back when he heard a scream behind him.

He turned quickly. At the intersection a young kid was lying in the street holding his leg. A car had screeched to a stop.

"You hit him! You fuckin' ran over him!"

An enraged bystander was pounding on the windshield of the car. Inside Raj could see the startled face

of a middle-aged guy dressed in a topcoat, a suburban-
ite from Rockaway coming to the city to stare at the
lights. He looked frightened and hesitant, but he
couldn't run if he wanted to. The crowd pinned his car
in tight. A trail of angry horns sounded in the dark
behind him.

"Let me through. I'm a doctor." Raj was kneeling
next to the fallen boy now. "Take your hand away. I
need to feel your foot. I'm not going to hurt you." The
boy moaned and squirmed, still holding tight.

"Lie still. You need to let me do this," Raj said. He
felt people at his back. One of them jostled hard
enough to push him over.

"Hey!" Raj yelled, catching himself with both hands
on the cold, wet street. When he looked up again, there
was a blank space in front of his eyes. The injured boy
had jumped up and darted off. Raj could see him just
for an instant before he melted away. *Ah.*

"You all right, buddy?" someone asked. "The light's
turned." Raj shook off a helping tug at his elbow. The
suburban driver was gone, too. Raj got up and started
running, fast. The kid was out of sight, but he couldn't
have gotten far.

It was treacherous weaving through huddled bodies
on the slippery sidewalk. Raj thought he saw the other
one, the guy who had posed as the angry bystander, but

maybe it wasn't him. The next light flashed "Don't Walk," which he ignored. It was the right move. Just ahead he spied both of them. Instinct told the kid that Raj was after him. He looked once over his shoulder and kept running.

Raj put on a burst, his lungs burning, and caught up. Grabbing the kid by the collar, he spun him around.

"You or him? Give it back!" he shouted. The kid's buddy had stopped ahead about a dozen feet. Raj pointed at him. "I'm taking your friend to the cops unless you give it back, you hear?"

The buddy, who looked to be around fifteen, hesitated a fraction of a second and then voted with his feet.

"Aw, man! He my cousin, too," the boy whimpered. He started to cry.

Raj said. "I just want my wallet back."

"I don't got it," the boy wailed.

"Then you're going to talk to a cop," said Raj, starting to pull the kid away. His adrenaline was up, but he noticed how light and frail the boy felt under his hand. Maybe he wasn't even twelve.

"Naw, mistah, please!" After some fumbling, the wallet was produced. The moment Raj touched it, the kid wriggled hard to break free.

"I can't get in no trouble," he cried. "My family! This is my first time, I swear."

He looked so scared and pathetic that Raj might have let him go. But he realized something.

"You've got a future in this," said Raj. "I mean, I never expected a kid to be such a pro." The kid quit crying as if a switch had been turned off. He waited for Raj's next move with suspicion.

"I don't have to look in this wallet, do I?" asked Raj. "Your buddy got the money out before he made the pass. Slick." The kid tried not to smirk—he still had to escape.

"We left you the cards. We too young for 'em," the kid said.

"I doubt it."

Raj held tighter to the boy's collar and peered inside his wallet. No cards.

"I was having a good evening before we met," Raj mumbled. "I guess you wouldn't care."

The boy, no longer squirming, made a calculation. Fearing the cold a lot less than the police, he slipped out of his baseball jacket and almost made it, but Raj was too quick and held him tight around his scrawny shoulders. He spun the boy around, and now his captive really did look frightened, his eyes wide and dilated.

Make him pay. The revenge impulse was hard to resist. He looked into the kid's eyes, and past the fear he saw a hardness that felt no pity for him. Only, there was

something else. Deeper than the hardness was someone
Raj knew. A person flickered through the haze, like
summer lightning through clouds, and he heard a silent
voice.

Don't you see me? Don't you? said Molly's voice.

"You look kinda sick," the kid said. Or perhaps it was
someone passing by. Raj had an uncanny feeling; it did
make him faintly sick.

Did you think I was only in you?

Yes, Raj thought. *If you can't come back for good, I want
you inside me. We love each other. That's what put you in me.*

Molly didn't answer. Raj had set out to find *It,* and
here *It* was. Wrapped inside a crummy, skinny kid with
felonious intent.

The kid said, "If you're gonna puke, don't do it on
me." But his voice was far away. Raj let him go. Now he
faintly saw Molly, like a candle through the shadow of
the kid's body. The candle grew brighter, as if it would
burst through entirely. Raj felt a stifled sob. Maybe he
looked so weak that the kid wasn't afraid anymore.
Instead of running he backed off a few feet and stood
his ground. Molly stood alongside him.

Raj held out his hand. The kid, misinterpreting,
scooted off at a fast trot. Molly didn't run away, but the
candle flickered out.

Wait.

Raj wanted to call after her, but he knew it made no sense. *It* was not running away with the boy but losing its soft focus, dissolving into vapor and memory. Raj tilted his head back to the cold, dark sky, now filled with a faint awe. There was silence about him, and he became aware of snowflakes, pinpoints of purity in the urban air, alighting on his face. Then a passerby elbowed him, and it was over.

M AYA LOOKED BOTH happy and troubled to see him as she opened her door and pulled him inside.

"I got worried waiting," she said.

Raj had arrived on time, even with the interlude in Times Square, but as he was rounding the corner to Maya's place, something had made him stop. The familiar world was wobbling away; that was clear enough. Another world might be beckoning to him. Would Maya recognize and accept this? Would she be willing to follow? After a time he knew he couldn't keep her waiting any longer, but he still hadn't answered himself.

"What have you been doing?" Maya asked. She seemed at ease and had kissed him at the door, but Raj could tell she didn't want to engage in his strange discoveries.

"Semi-foiling a criminal," Raj said. "A child criminal, actually."

Maya peeled off his leather jacket. "Let me run a hair dryer over this. You don't want it ruined," she said, heading for the bathroom. "I didn't know anyone could be semi-foiled."

"I managed it."

Raj eased himself onto the edge of the sofa so he wouldn't soak the upholstery "I had to walk—I didn't have any money," he said. Maya appeared running a blower over his jacket.

"Criminals can have that effect on a person. I'm very glad you're here. Barry's not going to be able to handle this thing at all, and Sasha is only making it worse."

"How?"

Maya didn't answer directly. "In Sasha's condition, could she get violent?" she asked.

"Depends. I take it she's threatened Barry?" said Raj. "Or is it worse than that?"

"It could be worse. It's not totally clear. Maybe you'd call it harassment. She won't leave him alone, and she shows up at all hours. Not always dressed like a lady. Maybe not dressed, period."

Raj said, "Sasha is paranoid. She's not going to handle distress normally. She might get intensely afraid, and at other times her fear might snap into rage."

"I see." Maya bit her lip and turned away. Raj looked around. Maya's room was hastily thrown together, but she had tossed a square of red silk over a table lamp, and Raj could smell patchouli.

He said, "Keep this in mind about Sasha. There's always going to be some element of suspicion. Don't expect her to trust you."

"She was starting to," said Maya.

"No, not really. Her disease won't permit that." Raj had been half-floating when he walked in, but not now. Being called on to use his training had pulled a corner of his life back under control. He could feel twinges of regret as he came back down to earth—it was like watching a far shore recede into the invisible.

Maya turned off the blower and handed his jacket back to him. She seemed hesitant and sad now. Quickly they left her place and went to the NYU dorms. On Barry's floor a few more lightbulbs had burned out in the hall, and a few more archaeological layers had been added to the litter. A beefy-looking man in uniform was knocking at Barry's door. Campus security.

"Is he in?" asked Raj.

"He's takin' a minute to hide some things," the man said tolerantly.

The door opened and Barry stood there. He looked as uneasy as he had the last time Raj had met him; he was wearing the same pajamas, too. "Whassup?" he mumbled automatically.

"Your complaint was put on file," the cop said. "I was just checkin'. She been comin' around any?"

Barry shifted his gaze. "It's cool," he said. "Are they with you?"

The cop looked over at Raj and Maya. "Never met 'em. So you're okay? I'm goin' upstairs to check on the lady, but otherwise we're leavin' it to you." In other words, Barry's parents would be called if he made any more official noise. Taking the boy's silence for the end of their exchange, the campus cop started to leave.

"Hold on," said Raj. "I'd appreciate it if you'd let us come with you. I'm the girl's doctor."

The cop shrugged indifferently. Raj faced Barry, who was in the familiar posture of closing the door in his face. "We need to talk," he said.

"You wish."

The door clicked shut and locked. Barry had successfully protected his cave.

The campus cop led them to Sasha's room and pounded on the door. There was no noise from inside. He waited another minute and called out, "Miss?" When no one answered, he pulled out a set of keys and unlocked the door.

The room was a shambles, bearing no resemblance to

the obsessive neatness Raj had seen last time. The dresser
drawers looked like they had exploded, the remains of old
meals perched here and there. The cop didn't look fazed.

"You should get a load of the boys' rooms," he said.
"I guess I don't really have cause to be here. I'll leave it
with you, doc."

Raj was about to say something, but Maya lifted a
finger. When the campus cop was well out the door, she
signaled for him to move quietly to the corner of the
room.

Silently Raj mouthed, "Why?"

Maya shook her head, then she sat down in the now
silent room, clearing some rumpled clothes off a chair.

"No one else is here. It's me. I hope you remember,"
she said.

The room didn't answer. A long moment passed. "A
lot of scary things have been happening. I know, and I
can help. Can you tell me if you understand?"

There was no more than a ruffle at one corner of the
bedspread, and maybe not even that. Slowly Maya got
down on her hands and knees. The brown stain was still
on the carpet, although someone had removed the cone
of dirt. She peered into the shadows under the bed
frame.

"I'm going to move closer," she said softly. "It's okay."

The darkest shadow seemed to quiver. Laying flat on the floor, Maya sidled under the bed. Raj knelt down to see where she went. His eyes adjusted and revealed Sasha curled up around a dirty pillow. She was dressed, and although her hair looked stringy and lank, she didn't appear to have deteriorated.

"I'm going to come a little bit closer," said Maya.

The girl didn't answer, but she lifted a hand to wipe her nose, and then she sneezed. From what he could see, Raj was relieved; Sasha didn't look as if she had been under there for days.

"I guess you heard us at the door," Maya said gently.

"No one wakes the princess," said Sasha. She sneezed again and began to crawl out on her own. Raj got to his feet and gave her a hand. Under the baggy jeans and sweatshirt she was beginning to show.

"Everyone's gone. It's just us," said Raj. Sasha mumbled and padded to the bathroom. Through the crack of the door Raj saw her washing her face. A good sign.

Maya crawled out, too, and said, "Are you hungry, Sasha? Can I get you anything?"

Sasha came out holding a plastic pill bottle. "Good girl," she said.

"Yes, I see you've been taking them," said Raj.

Sasha nodded and went back. The toilet flushed. She

emerged running her fingers through her hair. She was carrying an empty glass with two toothbrushes sticking out. Raj had the impression that she was about fifty percent there.

He said, "Have you told anyone about the baby yet? Pretty soon you'll need to see a doctor every week."

"I don't have to," said Sasha, flatly in her dull voice.

"You sort of do," Raj told her. "There's going to be two of you, and your baby needs help."

Sasha took this in slowly. "You can help," she said.

"Sure, some of the time, but you also need a baby doctor."

"No one but you," she insisted, raising her voice. Her face contorting, Sasha slammed the glass down on the table, then swiped her palm across her mouth, leaving a long smear of saliva.

"Okay," said Raj. "But if Maya fetches you, will you come to the hospital tomorrow?"

"Just you," Sasha repeated. "Or I'll kill you."

Whoa.

Raj tried not to jump, but his mouth went dry. "Have you felt like hurting anyone recently?" he asked quietly.

"And in the snow the mice would go because when water is frozen they cannot row," said Sasha in a high singsong voice. Raj took this as a yes.

"Have you been angry with Barry?" he asked.

"Six feet deep," said Sasha. At least she had the presence of mind to associate his name with "bury," although Raj didn't feel all that comforted. He took her hand to calm her. Maya pulled out a handkerchief, and wetting it, she wiped the saliva from Sasha's cheek.

A memory came back: Raj saw Maya, that day in the ward, months before, as she wiped lipstick from Sasha's mouth. Strange. This girl had a way of turning into an infant. An easy way to pull people in, but a hard way to live.

As quickly as she had flared, Sasha calmed down again. She gazed at the snow falling outside, humming a little to herself, and she squeezed Raj's hand tenderly.

"We have heard the chimes at midnight," murmured Sasha softly.

That we have, thought Raj. When Sasha turned drowsy, he let her lie down and then left with Maya. They went downstairs silently.

"She's not all right," said Maya.

"We have to do something," Raj replied. "Something extraordinary and quick."

They rode back to Maya's apartment house in a cab. As he let her off, Raj felt she wanted him to come up. Her tenderness with Sasha had left a deep impression. Raj wondered how he had ever let there be a conflict between her and Molly. Much remained to wonder about, even now. He reassured Maya that he would be back soon.

"I won't forget tonight," she said. "I feel like we're together again."

Raj watched her go up the steps. For now, he had more to say to the night than to her.

12.

Raj knew he was living on the edge of the impossible. A cool silence surrounded everything. The miraculous seemed close enough to touch. He might be holding a withered arm to take the pulse of a moribund old woman when suddenly he had to fight the urge to reach up and smooth away her wrinkles with his fingers.

Habib passed him in the hallways. "How's the air up there?" he asked.

"What?" Raj was barely sure he knew who was speaking to him.

"Nothing. Just don't get sucked out of the building."

With Christmas a few days away, Raj went to his mailbox in the residents' lounge and found a long, thin envelope. It didn't surprise him when he read the notice contained inside.

"Don't call it a dismissal," Halverson said when Raj confronted him. "It's not even a suspension."

"Is this because of one case you think I bungled? Or is it because I walked out of your office without asking permission?" Raj demanded.

Halverson looked uneasy. "We had to balance the interests of the clinic and your own situation. If you take a month's administrative leave now, you can make it up next summer. I don't expect you to be grateful right at this moment—"

"Really?" Raj interrupted.

"—but you might be when your judgment returns."

What it boiled down to was that Raj would be gone after New Year's, and he had a suspicion that getting back in would require a new evaluation and a pledge to fly right this time. He wouldn't pass and he knew it. He went directly from Halverson's office to a phone and called Maya. Raj wanted her with him for the holidays, but he also knew that she had to decide whether she could live in his new world with him.

"Your parents do Christmas?" Maya asked dubiously.

"They started giving me presents as a kid so I wouldn't be left out, and it just kept on. I can't quite explain," Raj said.

"Are you really asking me, or—?"

"Or what?"

"Or am I a stand-in for someone who can't be there?"

Raj didn't want to evade any longer. "Molly will be there. That's just how it is."

"Because you want it that way?" asked Maya.

"I'm not putting her between us," said Raj, "however it might seem. Just spend more time with me, and see if I'm what you want, even with this going on."

Reluctantly Maya accepted but was too busy to talk, she said. Hanging up, Raj knew that he was asking her to step outside the circle. Going out with him was one thing; conspiring to keep his secret was another. He was now a spook, someone looking for a revelation in his next Diet Coke or suture kit. He might float away, or something amazing could be at hand. Somehow the puzzle would converge, if he trusted.

Later that afternoon, with his dismissal note crumpled in the pocket of his white coat, Raj joined grand rounds. Trailing a group of other interns and residents, he went from room to room without commenting on any of the patients. The attending physician who was conducting the rounds, a Chinese neurologist named Dr. Ho, led them to the last room.

In one corner a gurney had been set up with an older woman lying stretched out. Pale and stiff, she didn't turn her head and appeared to be heavily sedated. Beside her stood Mathers.

"How is she doing?" said Ho, not bothering to ask the patient herself. "Are you ready to present?"

Mathers nodded. "Mrs. Berg is fine. No problems in prep," he said.

Ho reviewed the orders. "Given the light sedation, why is this patient immobile and unresponsive?" he asked the group.

"She looks catatonic to me," someone responded.

"That's partially justified," said Ho. "But look." He lifted the woman's arm and let it drop. "You'll note that the limb is not rigid enough for catatonia." Taking a long pin from his pocket, Ho pricked her lightly along her leg. "And we observe light twitching. Continue, Doctor."

Mathers read from his notes, "Mrs. Berg has consistently presented as a chronic depressive since early adulthood. She is unresponsive to drug therapies. It was decided early on to try electroconvulsive therapy, ECT. She has received twenty courses of shock over the years without much benefit."

Raj was half-listening. He slid around the back of the group until he was nearest to the woman, who could have been a corpse except for the faint rise and fall of her chest.

"When did she deteriorate?" asked Ho.

"We're not sure," said Mathers. "Her grown children found her sitting in a chair on Monday."

"Was she alert?" asked Ho.

"She was staring at the TV with an empty tray of frozen tacos in her lap. Apparently she didn't notice that the TV tube had burned out," Mathers said.

They're going to make her worse. Raj had been waiting for Molly's voice, and now it appeared. *She wants to die.*

Mathers placed his hand on Mrs. Berg's forehead. "We're going to try another shock today. Several consults have been called in on the case, and no one is a hundred percent, but the family wants something to happen."

"Sounds fairly routine," someone remarked at the other end of the group. Mathers waited for Ho to comment, although it was unlikely that he had a lot of either praise or criticism to offer. Mrs. Berg was seventy-three, and no one could see putting her on a couch to talk about a life that was heading downhill rapidly.

Give me a little time alone with her, said Molly.

That's impossible, thought Raj. They were going to wheel the patient away as soon as rounds were over. But he could feel Molly's urgency.

Raj spoke up as the group started to leave. "Why not leave her alone?" he said. "She hasn't responded well to ECT for decades. This seems pointless."

"I disagree," said Mathers. "It is well documented that in this kind of involutional psychosis, where the patient is elderly and onset is sudden, shock works. Even if it doesn't, it's still our best chance."

No. Molly's voice was insistent now. Raj felt it without knowing what he was supposed to do. All the other patients had been ones he could talk to. Mrs. Berg hadn't belonged in that category since her TV died.

"From what I can tell, your method is essentially a total failure," Raj argued, stalling for time.

Mathers turned to him. "I wouldn't go that far," he said.

"Then which part of her treatment would you consider successful so far?" asked Raj. "The depression that never went away, the fried part of her cortex that probably can't remember her children's names reliably, or maybe just the nightmares that bring up shame because she had to be shocked—what did you say? Twenty courses? That's about a hundred and thirty times!"

Mathers stared at him. "You don't know any of that for a fact. What are you basing this on?"

Raj didn't get a chance to answer. He was pushing two interns aside and leaning over the rigid, unseeing woman. *What are you doing?* he thought, because it wasn't him but Molly who now put both his hands on either side of Mrs. Berg's temples.

Hold on. I'm doing what I have to.

The group stirred uneasily. "Please back away from the patient," Ho said firmly. When Raj didn't move, Ho nodded to Mathers, who pulled at his arm.

"Get away," Raj snapped, throwing his arms back. He immediately put his hands on her temples again. He had no sensation of anything happening.

"I don't know what kind of ride you're on, but you don't get to take patients with you," said Mathers angrily. He grabbed Raj's shoulders and wheeled him around.

"What is all this?" a deep voice said. Halverson, who had been standing in the doorway, walked into the room. Bodies parted to let him get close to the gurney. Raj faced him, his eyes faintly dazed.

"Will you answer my question?" Halverson demanded.

"This woman has been subjected to over a hundred and thirty shocks that have done her absolutely no good. I was trying to prevent another," Raj said. He spoke quietly, without defiance. But it hardly mattered what he said. Mrs. Berg opened her eyes and sat up.

Halverson took two steps back, then he grabbed the chart from Ho's hand as the attending doctor gaped.

"I want to go home, please," said Mrs. Berg in a quavering voice. "The girl said I could."

"What girl?" said one of the interns.

"She's delusional," another remarked.

"Cancel the procedure and have this patient in my office in thirty minutes," Halverson ordered abruptly. Raj was already walking away.

"Come with me," Halverson said. When he had pulled Raj out into the hallway, he looked at him with an unreadable expression. "I've never witnessed anything like that in my entire professional career. That woman is alert again. What was your interaction with her before these grand rounds?"

"We've never met," said Raj.

"And you're telling me the whole truth? You brought her out of near catatonia with a touch? Do you practice faith healing?"

"You'd be making a mistake to think I did this," Raj said. He pulled free of Halverson and began to walk away. Out of the corner of his eye, he saw Claudia's room. The door was open; one of the student nurses was making up the empty bed.

"Come back. This is remarkable. We have to talk," Halverson called after him.

"There's nothing to talk about," said Raj. It was the moment when he knew for certain that he no longer belonged among the Matherses and Halversons. Stepping onto the elevator, Raj felt only the slightest hesitancy, because he didn't know if Claudia had gotten better or had just been sent away on another weekend pass.

A BITTER WIND hit the city, the kind that penetrates like an X ray. Looking down on the street in his bathrobe, Raj could see people clutching themselves to keep their skeletons from rattling. Maya had borrowed a car and was coming around for him. His family's Christmas party was tonight.

The phone rang. Raj left the bedroom and headed for it. "Hello?"

At the other end was one of those robotic voices:

This is AT&T. You have a collect call from—caller, please state your name.

"Princess bride." The voice was almost too faint to pick up.

Will you accept the charges?

"Sasha, is that you?" Raj said.

Will you accept the charges?

"Yes," barked Raj. "Jesus."

While he waited for the robot to cheerfully thank him, Raj had a sinking feeling. Two words can transmit a lot of desperation. If Sasha was feeling sane and had a reason for calling, she would have given her name.

"Hello?" Raj said, trying to sound relaxed, but the line went dead.

Maya pulled up fifteen minutes late in a gray sedan. Raj, who had been crouching in the doorway, jumped in quickly to escape the howling wind. She didn't lean over, so he took the initiative and kissed her. "You look nice," he said.

"I feel funny," said Maya.

"It's going to be okay."

"That's not what I mean." She put the car in reverse and backed up to the narrow alley that ran beside his building. "I thought I saw somebody in there."

Raj didn't need any more hints. "It's Christmas Eve and it's Sasha. I'm pretty sure."

Maya's voice cracked. "God, I couldn't feel more sorry for her, but—"

"Don't. We can't find her tonight," Raj said.

"That's not it," said Maya. She shook her head with a flinging motion and hunched down over the steering wheel. "Is this damn situation the only way we'll ever be together? She's not our sick baby."

Raj leaned over and kissed her again. "You mustn't worry right now," he said softly.

"You said we had to do something, but it's slipping away. And you with it," said Maya, on the brink of tears.

"No, it won't happen," said Raj. "We're together, and you're right, she's not our sick baby. I can call a crisis center from my parents' house." Maya, turning her head in his direction, seemed to accept what he was saying.

Raj put his hand over hers. "We can just stay in, the two of us alone," he said.

"Really?" said Maya. She sat up straight, shaking her head. She was still upset, but she could look at herself in the mirror and muster a weak smile. "We can't do that to your parents," Maya said.

DADDY-JI OPENED THE door so fast he might have been standing guard behind it. He threw himself around Raj.

"My boy, my boy." He was almost gasping with relief. "I couldn't live with myself if you missed the punch. Amma, it's all right!" he called over his shoulder.

Raj had no idea their worry had been so desperate. A couple of rooms away he could hear the last-minute whir of a blender as his mother ground the coconut chutney with mint and green chili.

"Say hello to Maya," Raj said when he could unwrap a tentacle. "Stay with my father. He goes kind of nuts."

"Nonsense, what a thing to say! I'm just in high spirits. We all should be." Daddy-ji took a swing into jollity. "You are a beautiful girl. We are thrilled to have you in our home again. Even if it took this rascal to bring you."

While Maya smiled and nodded, Raj headed for the kitchen to find Amma. She was standing quietly by the stove waiting for him, as was her style. She said, "So, it's you, I think. Do I recognize you?"

She turned her cheek to be kissed. Raj looked closely at his mother, who was specially painted and coiffed for him. She had applied too much makeup—she was like a doll in rouge and henna—but he was touched.

Raj said, "Have you added the pistachios yet?" This referred to the special ingredient, the royal touch, that Amma added to her holiday dish of rice *biryani*.

"Of course not. Don't I always wait for you?"

Raj kissed her again. It was easy to fall into his accustomed role of returning prince. It brought his parents happiness, and this year it would assuage his guilt for forgetting them.

"Maya, come in here!" Raj cried. "Prepare to be amazed."

In five minutes it was all lovingly unreal. Maya was allowed to stir the *makhani* sauce and ooh over the roast pheasant. Raj would tell her later about Daddy-ji's slightly cracked love of English manners. His own father, Raj's grandfather, had been a steward in a gentleman's club in Bombay, and even after Independence, the family held fast to his standards of gentility. Then there was the punch.

"Try, try," Daddy-ji urged. He thrust a glass into Maya's hands. "You'll never guess."

"Vodka, yogurt, and rose water," said Raj, who had come into the living room where the punch bowl stood on a sideboard that was covered in white silk with the goddess Devi printed all over in gold. "I peeked over his shoulder one year."

"But you don't know the real secret, I can tell you that," exclaimed Daddy-ji. "Drink up, girl, I have never seen anyone so young and luscious under my roof!" For a man who never drank, he was already half-tossed. Maya burst out laughing but downed her glass.

"Don't mind him," Raj whispered in her ear. "It's just the rose water talking."

He let the evening glide on, only breaking away to find the phone in the bedroom. The hospital had no record in the ER of anyone who fit Sasha's description. On a hunch, he tried the dispensary at the university.

"And that's all you can tell me?" he said. "Do you understand that she could be in real danger? All right, it's not up to you. Good night."

Raj hung up and heard Maya enter the room behind him. "They stonewalled me," he said. "Confidentiality, plus no one is allowed to see Sasha's records without her parents' permission."

You'll find her.

Raj whipped around. Molly was standing by the bed. "We did pretty good this afternoon at the hospital," she said and sat down beside him. "So that's it, I guess."

Raj's heart raced. "That's what?" he mumbled, afraid of her answer.

"Your ghost story."

Molly was wearing the black dress Raj had chosen for her for the funeral, which frightened him more than her words.

"It's just an outfit," said Molly, smiling.

"You can't leave me. I don't know where to go. I don't know what I'm fit for anymore," Raj pleaded.

"You're fit to love Maya," said Molly. "You made your choice this evening."

"How can that answer everything?" Raj protested. *It's where this all started,* he thought hopelessly.

Molly said, "Here, lie back." They rested on the muslin-covered bed, and Raj held her. He only felt his tears after they began to evaporate and made his cheeks cold. Molly's first words when she returned had been, "Prove to me that you won't cry." She would have to live with the disappointment.

"You're going to be a healer," Molly said softly. "This afternoon at the hospital showed what could be done. Maybe you won't ever walk back into that world, but there are other places. You'll find them."

Raj couldn't listen. It seemed that the heart of his heart would break. Then Molly drew him in so that they were both sitting on the bed.

"Look," she said, pointing to the wrinkled muslin sheets.

Molly's pale hand moved over the hills and valleys of cotton, the fine kind from India that one could almost see through.

Molly said, "You think I came into your life and then left. But I didn't. These hills and valleys are like individual lives. They seem to be separate, yet if you look again, they belong to one unity. That unity is love. We rise into this life to express only love. We come here to know who we are. We crave the bliss of our being. Only those things are real.

"I told you I made a bargain to come back," said Molly quietly. "But I didn't come back as a person. The person you see is just a dim form of reality. Death releases us from that mirage."

"What are you, then?" asked Raj.

"Just keep looking." Raj took his eyes from Molly's face and gazed back at the rumpled sheet, with its creases and folds. Molly squeezed the material and let it drop.

"New folds and creases appear, but you can't say that they were born or that the old hills and valleys died. They are all movements in this one reality that is eternal love, a sea of being that contains everything. Our hopes raise us up; our despair pulls us down. But we can never be separate from love. All events, all things, all relationships are movements of love, throwing up new forms without end."

"Then what about pain and suffering?" asked Raj.

"Some of the creases get cramped, but they will eventually be smoothed away. Love knows. It understands every impulse anyone has ever had, and even though suffering occurs, love prevails."

"Can you expect someone dying alone in pain to accept this?" asked Raj.

"In time. It takes a journey of countless experiences to understand, but when you die, you see the truth immediately; there is no question. Love. Knowingness. Bliss. Everything else flows from them."

Raj looked down, and the muslin began to shimmer as if it were woven of light. The wrinkles became ripples of light, lasting mere seconds. He saw then that his own life was just as fleeting and impermanent. All grasping was in vain. All clinging was futile. But there was no fear in dying because the next second was birth; renewal was forever and now at the same time.

There was only one question left. "Who are you, really?" he asked Molly.

"I am love. I don't think you ever made a mistake about that," she said smiling.

Whether Molly had taken ten minutes or a fraction of a second, Raj didn't know. However, in those few moments he suddenly saw that their lives—Molly's, Maya's, and his—had been intertwined for lifetimes. They had endured privation together and fled from war, starved on barren plains and worshiped deities without number. In the swollen tide, they had never drifted apart, no matter how often they seemed to lose sight of one another. Every new beginning was joyful; every ending raised the possibility of hope.

He could hear the sharp rattle of windowpanes as the wind tried to force itself in. As the room became more solid, Molly changed. Raj couldn't touch her anymore; she barely held the form of a woman. She became the shimmering light and disappeared.

He felt a light touch on his shoulder. "Raj?"

Maya was in the room holding a glass of punch. Raj's glance was pulled to his hand. He was still holding the phone.

"They wouldn't tell me anything," he heard himself say, still feeling far away. "But I think Sasha was there today. I'm going to check in person as soon as I can."

By the time he'd finished, the room was back in focus, and Raj could look up and see Maya without feeling that he had evaporated.

"Now?" Maya asked.

Raj shook his head, laying the phone down. "There's only a nurse on duty tonight. It will have to wait until morning. Come on."

He pulled Maya back into the living room where Daddy-ji and Amma were seated at a round table pulled into the center of the room. They were trying not to exchange glances. Raj broke the ice with a compliment and a toast. The rest of Christmas Eve was merry if you didn't think too hard about the wind that never stopped trying to break into the house, and someone out in it.

On the way home, the car was filled with the gentle tension of now or never. If this made Maya nervous, she didn't show it. She had taken Raj's hand under the table after dinner, when Amma brought out the spiced, steaming *chai*.

Now she said, "It's a lot to accept. Everything's going to feel different."

"Maybe better," said Raj.

"I'm not sure I can bring it around to that," said Maya, wanting to believe him.

"Then it doesn't have to be better," said Raj. "Make it that I'm a face you've seen a thousand times in a thousand places. You are that for me, and so is Molly. If anyone finds a soulmate, their love has to exist beyond faces and masks and bodies. You won't have me until you see through Raj. I won't have you until I see through Maya. Is that possible for you?"

"You're asking me to be extraordinary," said Maya.

"You are extraordinary. That part isn't new," said Raj.

He made love to Maya downtown with red silk thrown over the lamp. They undressed quickly without talking, their clothes left where they fell. The beginning wasn't shy, but it wasn't a hurried rush, either. They moved as liquidly together as Raj had once moved with

Molly. Compared to her, Maya was less private; as soon as Raj lay down beside her, her embrace accepted him without holding back.

The ceiling thudded from the bass action of some dance music that was being blasted above them. Raj whispered, "It's like making love under an elephant."

Maya laughed and raised herself toward him again. As a lover she had a very light touch; she liked to smile, never seeming to sink into a gulf of passion but floating above it. A lover with nuance. None of this was wasted on Raj. He was alert and present as he had never been before. By the time they finished, the thudding had stopped, and Raj knew that it was Maya alone in bed with him.

He watched her fall asleep and would have wrapped himself around her, but at midnight Raj silently put on his clothes and went out. His instinct told him that if he wanted to slip through the cracks, it had to be now.

The pavilion was short-staffed this one night, and when he got off the elevator, Raj didn't recognize the nurse subbing at the station, who looked up indifferently and went back to her book. The door to Claudia's room was shut. Raj went in without knocking.

"Here," he said, holding out a paper bag.

Claudia wasn't asleep or even in bed but standing by the window facing out. She turned around. "For me?"

Raj took out a half-filled plastic soda bottle. "You won't like it much, not unless you're used to vodka and yogurt." He set the offering down on the bedside stand. Claudia didn't move toward it; she gave him a crooked smile.

"I know this isn't a truce, so what is it?" she asked.

Raj said, "I was riding back from a party. Everyone was pretty happy there, and I thought of one old bitch who probably wasn't."

"Oh yeah? I'm thinking someone didn't slap you hard enough when you were born," said Claudia, but tolerantly.

"I'm not going to be back for any more sessions," said Raj. "Partly thanks to you. So I took the liberty of explaining your case in a long note that's now in your chart."

Claudia approached the bottle and toasted him with it before taking a swig.

"Aren't you interested in what I wrote?" asked Raj.

"Not particularly."

Raj said, "I could have said that you are a borderline personality who is overwhelmed by feelings from the past and cannot handle them without a mask of aggression. That would kind of fit."

"Bitch is a lot shorter. Is there perfume in this stuff?" Claudia asked.

"Essence of rose, in fact. I could also have noted that your sense of being victimized has made you so bitter that you no longer have a conscience. You trample everyone's boundaries as callously as yours were trampled in the distant past. Why else would you be flooded by feelings you can't remember and yet can't forget?"

Claudia tensed; she got past her distaste for the punch and took a long belt.

"I didn't write any of those things," said Raj. "I just put down one sentence. 'I have never met anyone who so deserves to be healed.'" Before Claudia could react, Raj stepped near the door and turned off the light, plunging the room into near darkness.

"Hey!" Claudia's voice was alarmed but quiet.

Raj walked over to her in the dark. He knew that if he was right, she wouldn't oppose him. He found the bottle in her hand and took it away. "Sit down now, and be still," he told her.

After a slight hesitation, she obeyed. Raj stood over the dim slumping form he could barely make out. Of all the secrets he had been keeping, there was a particular one that he had saved for this moment. His hands wavered up and around her, gently and slowly. In the soft brushing of the air, he felt her pain and the wall she threw up to keep from being humiliated by more pain. A tangle of feelings had suffocated her, year by year, until she faded into the background of life. None of this was a mystery to Raj. To be sensitive to a wounded being is not difficult.

The real secret was that these invisible strands of suffering could be undone. The gathering of pain wasn't invisible. It was there, like a dirty cocoon around her. Raj started pulling at them, and the strands started coming loose. It was easy, actually, once you saw the difference between a soul and the web that covers it. Strip a person of everything that can cause trouble, and what remains must be the soul.

"Doctor?" The substitute nurse was standing at the door. Her hand reached for the light switch, then hesitated. "Is this your patient?"

"I don't think she's anyone's patient anymore," Raj said. He turned on the light.

"All right, then. Sorry to barge in." The nurse left, no doubt to put a note on the chart, or to slip a piece of paper under Halverson's door. Claudia shivered slightly as she looked up.

"What did you do?" she whispered.

"Nothing," said Raj. "I'm going to write a discharge order for you, effective tomorrow morning. You won't be passed on to another doctor. This time you won't need to be."

Claudia yawned. "That's the worst punch with the

best kick I've ever drunk," she said. Raj lifted her legs into bed and waited the five minutes it took before she dozed off.

The next morning Raj located the young doctor at the NYU dispensary who had seen Sasha the day before.

"Messy business," he mumbled. Perhaps because Raj was also an Indian, he slacked a bit on the rules. "She was in an agitated state, but that's not why we wanted to admit her. I can't read her chart to you, but I think you can piece things together."

The young doctor's eyes glanced over to where a nurse practitioner was sewing up a basketball player's busted lip. It bled a lot, and there were a few smears of red on the table beside the boy's head. Raj realized that Sasha's blood had been there yesterday.

"The stress gets to them too much," the young doctor said.

"But you didn't admit her?" asked Raj urgently.

The young doctor shook his head. "No, the girl ran out too fast. I've put in a call to her parents, but I only got their machine. Security has been alerted to keep watch on her room if she comes back. I shouldn't be telling you this much."

Raj thanked him and left. It was the clearest Christmas morning he could remember, and falling on a

Sunday, the thin traffic had not been able to smudge the freshness in the air or the sparkling sky. Raj walked across campus, faintly expecting to spot Sasha. One way or another it was over, however. The dispensary would now register her as a suicide attempt, which would bring the family in whether they wanted it or not. The news would give enough people the jitters that Sasha wouldn't be welcomed back at school, either, Raj guessed.

There was only one more place the trail might lead. Raj took a cab and showed up at Serena's door. When he knocked, a loud voice shouted, "Come in."

Raj stepped into the living room. In one corner, a skimpy tree was leaning, the kind left over at the lot when you forget to buy early enough. Directly in front of him Sasha was facing Serena. Both were on their feet.

"Nothing can stop the night!" Sasha shouted. She was wearing sweat pants and a torn shirt, her hair lank and dirty. Serena reached out to calm her, but Sasha jumped away. She didn't even register that Raj was in the room.

"We're going to have to sit you down," Serena said in a measured voice. "Turn around. Look who's here."

Sasha started to scream in a high, shattering wail. She held her arms out in a crucifix pose, her head tilted back.

Serena and Raj pounced at the same time. They moved in from either side to seize an outstretched arm. Sasha writhed and kicked in manic desperation. Serena was having a hard time with her side.

"I can't inject her without my bag," said Raj urgently. "Find some rope or a torn-up sheet. Let her go, I think I can hold her."

Serena nodded and released Sasha's arm. Raj pulled downward while slipping his foot behind Sasha's kneecap, hoping to throw her off balance. Instead the girl broke free, and when Raj looked up, she was holding a gun. The silver barrel pointed straight at his chest.

"Jesus, Jesus, this I know, for the Bible tells me so," Sasha keened. Holding her arms out straight before her, she exposed her wrists, which were wrapped in bandages stained with old blood.

At that frozen moment it made no sense for Raj to feel anything but panic. Instead he calmly looked in her eyes and saw what Sasha couldn't. That crazy mask wasn't her. The flood of pain that carried her away wasn't her. Without Molly to guide him, Raj saw a shifting, shimmering light, not visible but of the soul. At every second the light reaches deep, trying to call everyone out. Raj could see that this didn't just apply to him or Molly or anyone who longs to be awakened. The light pierces suffering and pain. It was the invisible presence that made the point of the gun sacred, and the hand holding it.

Without saying "put down the gun," Raj told himself that she would, because she would be able to see herself now through his eyes. He waited. Sasha faltered. She could end it there, as her voices told her, with another terrified dash into darkness.

"Tiddley-boo," Sasha said.

Serena had frozen in place ten feet to her left. "What are you waiting for?" she said in a steady voice, looking Raj in the eye. "Let her take you out. Or are you staying for lunch?"

"You're putting this on me?" said Raj. "I could die here."

"I've got news for you, honey. Someone helped you get over that," Serena said.

The sound of their voices distracted Sasha. She lowered the gun a fraction, and Serena jumped, throwing her to the floor with the full weight of her body. She grabbed the gun from Sasha's hand.

"Ow!" Sasha yelled but quickly stopped struggling.

"No one's trying to hurt you," said Raj to reassure her. It took a moment more to carry Sasha over to the sofa. She slumped down, hanging her head. Her manic rage had turned to dull torpor.

No doubt Serena was right, Raj thought. It was on him. He had mysteriously arranged at that precise moment to get Sasha, crazed and schizophrenic, to shoot him so that he could join Molly. *You'll get what you want.* Serena had told him that already, when Raj had been so desperate.

"I'm glad you decided to stay after all," said Serena, reading his mind. "Welcome to the playground."

"Yeah." Raj was panting hard. He hadn't realized how much the adrenaline was flowing.

Raj called the hospital to arrange for Sasha to be committed on his orders. She remained far away, silent and dull during the ride back in Serena's car. It was several hours before Raj got free again, but Serena had waited. He asked her to drop him off at Maya's place.

"You think you could have saved her, don't you?" said Serena.

"I got distracted. But I'll have another chance," Raj said. He was certain of it. *Every soul wants to be seen,* he thought, *but some are more disguised than others.*

Before letting him off downtown, Serena said something surprising: "Let me die so I can be with the angels. Then I will ask the angels to let me die so I can be with the stars. After that, where I go, no one can imagine."

"What's that?" Raj asked.

"A poem. Take care of yourself."

Serena drove off in a twilight that looked as clear as the rest of the day had been. It was still early, but Venus could be seen suspended between two buildings to the west. Whatever lay beyond the stars, someone had come out to tell the secret.

From the Author

W HEN LOVE IS set free, it obeys no limits. It seeks
out the secret places that never hoped to feel loved, and
once it touches them, the result is foreordained. Love will
win. The same is true for healing—they have this in common. Raj Rabban was incredibly fortunate to find one person who saw that he was meant to be a healer. He became
one because Molly looked at him with the eyes of the soul.

I couldn't let go of Raj after that, however. I kept
thinking about everyone who doesn't find a Molly.

Who never hears anyone say, "I am love." I wanted Raj to return in five years and gather everyone around to reveal how he kept on loving and healing. It would be very satisfying to the author if he said just a few things that could be remembered when hard times come and there is a drought of love:

Love isn't a mere sentiment. It contains truth, and therefore it is law.

Love conforms to our vision. You'll always get what you want, so have the desire for the highest love you can imagine.

The only perfect love is beyond the personal. If you want to give someone your greatest love, first see beyond that person. If you want to receive the greatest love, see yourself beyond the person.

Divine love exists. It is expressed through human beings.

The love that comes from your soul endures death.

Don't believe anything is more real than your soul.

If Raj told us these things, I believe they would be the truth, but never the whole story. No matter how many times you've felt it, love will always remain infinite and mysterious. Like God, love runs ahead of us, and just when we think we've caught up, it slips farther ahead.

Anything is possible, as Serena wrote on her map, so be prepared. And if you are the kind of reader who turns to the last page of a book first, the ending is love.

Always.

DEEPAK CHOPRA

The
DAUGHTERS
OF *JOY*

AN ADVENTURE OF THE HEART

PUTNAM